AF425184

WHISKY, WOMEN AND WORLD

TAHER AHMED

Made with ❤ on the Notion Press Platform
www.notionpress.com

Contents

Content Warning

This novel contains scenes involving alcohol consumption, characters who smoke, depictions of violence, discussions of domestic abuse, references to sexual violence, sexual content, explicit language, and themes related to transgender individuals and LGBTQ+ experiences. It is important to note that the portrayal of these elements is not intended to harm or depict any real-life individuals or communities negatively. Reader discretion is advised, and if any of these themes are sensitive or triggering for you, please consider your emotional well-being while reading.

I

The sun slowly rose in the east, its rays glimmering on the wet grass and leaves in the garden. The smell of freshly rained soil wafted through Kovalam, a coastal town in Kerala. It was a warm morning, the kind that followed a comfortable, rainy night. The garden leaves rustled softly with the gentle morning breeze, and the sky was a deep azure. The air was filled with a feeling of contentment, and the place seemed to hum with peaceful energy. Even the birdsong seemed softer than usual, as if it too was lulled into a peaceful trance by the calming atmosphere.

The girl stood by the rusted grill, gazing at her stepfather's scooter. The seat was dotted with droplets of rain. She was ready for school, her long black hair neatly oiled and braided with two pony tails on either side. Her blue school uniform was perfectly pressed. She silently waited until her stepfather emerged from the house. He stared back at her with a suspicious look on his face that made her feel uneasy. However, she did not waver from her stance. After wiping down his scooter with a dry cloth, he turned it on and started it up. She watched as the scooter slowly rolled away, hoping he would not return.

Gently, the girl grabbed her bag and made her way to the wardrobe, stuffing it with a pair of clothes. She then stepped into her stepfather's room and knew where he would hide his money. A roll of cash was hidden in his wrinkled shirt pocket, hanging behind the door. It weighed heavily, and she knew it was meant to pay the rent. In her attempt to find out if she was being watched, she was surprised to see her mother standing at the entrance of the room, her eyes focused on her daughter. The girl had been caught off guard, but accepted it and stood frozen. The look on her mother's face was not one of anger, but of acceptance. The mother stepped into the room, reached out and touched the pink slap mark left on her daughter's face. Tears slowly welled up in her eyes, and the daughter looked back sadly at the bruises on her mother's wrist. Both stood silent. They knew what had to be done. The mother took a deep breath and walked out of the room.

It was her last day at school and the atmosphere was filled with a mix of joy and anxiety. Everyone seemed excited for the upcoming holidays, but also had to face pressing exams that day. But the girl was confident about her knowledge and wasn't interested in chatting with other kids. She walked straight to her classroom and waited for her exam to start. Felt both excited and nervous, but ready to put her best foot forward and take on the challenge.

When the clock finally struck the end of the exam, there was a collective sigh of relief as everyone knew it was over. But the girl wasn't done yet and used the remaining time to double check her answers.

She stepped out of the school, deliberately avoiding interactions with her peers. She halted by a nearby auto rickshaw and got in, resolute in reaching her destination without any further delays. On her way, the girl changed her clothes at a public toilet. As she exchanged her school uniform for her regular attire, her heart sank, acknowledging that she would never wear this uniform again, and a profound sorrow engulfed her. She pushed the uniform into her bag and carried on with her journey.

The girl paid the bill to the rickshaw driver before entering the huge and crowded railway station. As she stepped in, the smell of the station filled her nostrils and the roar of the station made her heart race. She nervously walked through the throng of people towards the ticket counter, as directed by the woman sweeping the platform. She slowly shuffled through the queue, watching as the others ahead of her finally reached the counter. It took over half an hour for her turn to come. The man at the ticket counter glared suspiciously at her when she asked for a ticket with the next train about to leave. The girl was taken aback by the intensity of his gaze and her heart raced as she tried to keep her composure. The man eventually slid the tickets through the corroded grill.

Collecting the ticket, the girl walked away after pushing the crowded queue of people on either side. Her hands were shaking and her eyes darted around the station, searching for her train. She checked her ticket again and again to make sure she hadn't missed it; her fingers traced the words written in tiny black ink. Finally, she spotted the place she was looking for, and uttered the name of her destination with excitement and fear. Taking a deep breath, she smiled and moved closer to the platform, eager to embark on her journey.

II

My dark apartment once again bathed in the warm glow of light as I tightened the bulb and kicked the stool aside. I stood there for a while, gazing across the room, trying to acclimate to the greenish hue it now emitted. Previously, the room had been covered in a soft orange, reminiscent of sunshine. Now, it felt as if I were in a deserted bar where the chaotic human who loved to dance had forgotten to visit.

I removed my shirt and threw it on the bed, then walked over to my table to jot down one last thought. This idea occurred to me while purchasing the green bulb to replace the old one that had stopped working. I absentmindedly placed a cigarette between my lips, allowing it to dangle there, unlit. My fingers pressed down on the typewriter keys with determination, my touch gentling as I grew confident that I wouldn't forget this thought again. Finally, I settled on the open windowsill, which lacked any grills, and gazed out at the city that had fallen into slumber.

I contemplated how my apartment room must appear to an observer looking up at the building—just greenish rays streaming through a five-foot-four window, illuminating a man enjoying a cigarette. Then, I picked up my draft and began to read it slowly. Everything I had written over the past three hours sounded either pathetic or like an ambulance siren blaring in my ears.

When I finished reading the eight pages I had painstakingly composed, my frustration boiled over. I had to release my anger somehow, so I spat on the draft. Unsatisfied, I plucked the cigarette from my lips and started to burn the corners of the pages one by one. Some of the papers I let float into the air outside the window, where they twirled and danced in the wind, while others scattered within my room. The slowly smoldering pages resembled a lantern festival, albeit in reverse. The empty papers drifted downward, contrasting with the lanterns that soared high into the sky.

Frustrated and unsatisfied, I decided to numb my emotions with some liquor. The regular wine shop would be closed, and I was already running late. Fortunately, the one next to my apartment always catered to my needs, no matter the hour. All I had to do was kick the shutter, shout at the top of my lungs, or create a scene. Initially, the shopkeeper would respond with curses, but then, as he made his way to the window of his room on the first floor, he would greet and ask me to wait.

As with every other night, I requested a cheap whisky and handed over the cash. He rolled the bottle through the partially opened shutter and hastily closed it to avoid the prying eyes of the police. My tongue and body were accustomed to its taste, and I downed the entire bottle in less than ten seconds, standing in a narrow street behind the wine shop. I checked my pocket and was relieved to find enough cash for a few more bottles of whisky. "You're a wretched writer!" I muttered to myself as I once again kicked the shutter. That was the last thing I recalled from that fateful full moon night.

***

In the waning light of the setting sun, the sun's rays were still weak and faint, painting the sky in shades of pink and orange. I jolted awake to the sight of a car zooming past just a few inches from my hair. My heart thumped as I turned to my right to see the car screeching to a halt at the red light. Catching my breath, my gaze slowly wandered to the sky. The birds twittered and a tiny airplane flying off into the horizon. I looked around and quickly realized where I was. Lying on the sidewalk, in the middle of a busy city street, bustling with people, cars, and activity. I watched with my blurred vision as cars sped by, honking their horns, and people walked down the sidewalk, their conversations overlapping. The place was an absolute mess. The streets were filled with garbage and the air was thick with urine stench. Despite the municipality's efforts, it seemed like the filth was here to stay, as if it had become part of the landscape. Luxury cars drove past this mess with aplomb, their shiny exteriors glistening in the evening sun. Between this beauty and the mess, I lay there like another piece of garbage, realizing I had survived another day.

My head pounded and my mouth was dry. I had been out drinking the night before, and had no recollection of how I had ended up on the street. Embarrassment rushed my soul when I realized I was lying there half naked. A mother nearby desperately tried to distract her daughter from staring at me, but it was too late. The young girl looked at me with wide eyes, as I struggled to wake up and leave. Trying to put on my pajamas quickly, I stood up, my body aching and my movements sluggish. Ashamed of my behavior, I began walking to remain unnoticed and out of sight. However, I could feel passersby stare at my disheveled appearance as I kept my head down.

Walking down the street on my way to my apartment, I decided to buy a packet of cigarettes. I could feel the weight of the cigarettes in my pocket and it reminded me of how the disclaimer in the packet: *Smoking is injurious to health* has ironically helped me survive all these years. Despite all the warnings, I continued to smoke, as if my body was immune to smoking's adverse effects. Realized that the only thing that had not changed all those years was my smoking habit. The pungent smell of it was strangely comforting, and the smoke slowly soothed my hangover headache.

I lived in an apartment thirteen floors high, and it was quite a sight. The building was tall and imposing, but the most memorable thing about it was the rusted old lift. Every time I got inside, it made me nervous. It creaked and groaned and I wondered if it would reach the top. The lift walls were scratched and the handrails were corroded. The windows were so grimy it was almost impossible to see out. Still, I rode it up and down, day after day, and felt adventurous.

In this huge apartment, my space was barely large enough for a single bed, a desk, and chair. The walls were drab, and the floor was covered in dust and cobwebs from years of neglect. At the desk rested a typewriter, its keys yellowed with age. The chair is worn and frayed, threadbare from years of use. The mattress was covered with a wrinkled and faded blanket, and a single pillow, flat and without life. The corner of the room was piled up with boxes of papers, manuscripts of stories that were never published, their pages filled with hopes and dreams that never came true. Lying in the other corner was an old tape recorder, a relic of a bygone era. It played music automatically with no controls. If I tapped it repeatedly, it responded and stopped playing. Even stranger, it sometimes started humming in the middle of the night, its distorted melody filling the room. But strangely, I found comfort in its presence. The uninvited music was a blissful reminder of a simpler time.

I walked straight inside my filthy bathroom to pee and my eyes were glued to the dark sky outside through the window. Several tall buildings stretched into the heavens, almost touching the clouds. My stare was drawn from the clouds to the glass bowl placed near the window, filled with money plants floating in water. It was a small oasis amidst the dirt and grime of the bathroom with broken tiles and the faint smell of mildew.

I sat in the corner of the bed and lit another cigarette. The smoke filled my dark room, slowly wreathing and curling through the air. It seemed to linger, and it was difficult to ignore the acrid scent that came with it. Every now and then, a tendril of smoke would reach the window, where it would slip through the crack in the glass and drift away into the night. The whole scene was oddly calming until my eyes were directed towards my awards on the shelf. A feeling of revulsion ran through me as I thought about what I had become in the last two decades. My successes seemed paltry and meaningless now, a hollow reminder of my achievements. I felt a deep sense of disappointment in myself, knowing that I had done nothing to make a lasting impact on the world. All these awards provided me with fleeting moments of joy, which faded away with time. The thought of not completing a single successful story in the past two decades after being claimed as an inspiring writer in the Indian film industry once made my heart pierce with guilt and insecurities.

"What remains for me in this cruel world if the art within me has perished?" The thought provoked me to end my life. There was nothing left for me to live in despair, and I could not see a way out. All I wanted was to escape pain and suffering. The small amount of alcohol that helped me through my depression and writings has now consumed me like a plague and taken over my life. The creative spirit and observational powers I possessed as a writer were traded off to drink and stay afloat in the madness of this world. I felt like I was in a deep, dark hole with no way out.

I felt the pajamas tighten around my neck as I slowly dropped myself, my feet dangling in the air. Despite not knowing what lay ahead, I knew it was the right choice. The fan stopped screeching, and my life slipped away under the fan engine pressure. As life drained out of me, I was thankful for the peace I finally found. Slowly I closed my eyes and welcomed the darkness that embraced me. My journey had come to an end.

I was ready to leave this world and enter into another one, or perhaps its abyss. But, in the next few seconds, I stumbled to the floor with a heavy thud, the fan breaking off and taking me with it. A sharp pain shot through my leg and what appeared in the mirror was not a pleasant sight—my gray linen shirt was filled with vomit stains, and my pajamas were tied around my neck. As I lay there, I noticed a stream of blood trickling down my hairy thigh. This was a result of the fan blade cutting me in its fall. My eyes turned red and stretched wide as I tried to breathe heavily. Quickly, I untied the pajamas from my neck and drank a glass of water that soothed my throat. The sound of music came out of nowhere, like a ghost from the past. It was an old romantic song by Ilayaraaja. The song would have made me elated if I was not trying to kill myself, but at this moment, it felt like a cruel joke.

I knew I had to get out of this situation, but I didn't know how. Slowly, I tried to stand up and looked around. The room was empty and surrounded with deep, overwhelming loneliness. It was like a heavy weight pressing down on me, a suffocating stillness that sounded like it would never end. I felt utterly alone, as if no one in the entire world could understand me or what I was struggling with. Is this solitude or loneliness? My mind was filled with questions without answers, and sadness that seemed to never end. Taking a deep breath, I opened the door and walked out, lighting another cigarette.

***

I awoke the next morning to the bright summer sun streaming through my window. The air was crisp and clear, and the sun's rays seemed like an embrace. I felt the warmth on my back and the beads of summer sweat that formed as I slept. Took a deep breath and savored the scent of the freshly lit cigarette. Leaning out of my open window, I looked into Chennai's chaotic morning with a sense of exhilaration. The sun slapped my bare body, waking me up with its heat. I observed the city as it came alive again, starting another loop of humanity's never ending cycle. Cars whirred past, people bustled through the streets, and honking sounds filled the air. I felt a sense of wonder as I realized how small I was compared to the grandness of it all. Inhaled one last puff of my cigarette before flipping it in the air.

My tiny, filthy room always looked heavenly in the morning, when the sun's rays illuminated the dust particles in the air and gave off a gentle, shimmering gleam. At other times, it was dull and uninviting, lit only by the flickering of the tubelight or a bulb I had installed to create a bar-like atmosphere. Still, there was something about those mornings that made the room look beautiful. I savored those few moments of peace before the day's chaos began. At times I dance in the reflection of sun rays that move around my walls, creating an exquisite silhouette of my body. Or I find myself soaking in the sun's rays, tears streaming down my face for no apparent reason. But often I am in the mood to sit back and relax, and nothing could be better than listening to some of the timeless classics of Ilayaraaja. As I sit and listen to the soulful melodies, I take my eyes off the music and look vacantly at the mesmerizing patterns of sun rays dancing across my walls and ceilings. I'm captivated by the beauty of the moment and the hope that something so beautiful can last. In times like these, my loneliness becomes a comforting addiction. The presence of a crowd only amplifies the feeling of suffocation within me. I treasure moments like these, imprinting them in my memory. They embody a state of pure bliss, offering the serene respite I require from life's bustling chaos.

That morning, I was in no mood to shower, but all I needed was a cup of tea to get started with the day and its drama. I got dressed up, grabbed my laptop bag, and shoved my recently written draft in there. Everywhere I go, people stare at my face and scan my outfit disdainfully. I can feel them hesitating to stand next to me, taking a few steps back and then standing away. It's like I'm an infectious disease they don't want to catch. I never cared much for fashion, instead opting for comfort and practicality in my everyday wardrobe, which consisted of four loose-fitting linen shirts and two jeans bought a decade ago. My accessories included a large pair of glasses, without which I could barely see, and an expensive Rado watch with a cracked face. It stood as a symbol of cherished memories I never wished to lose, and

I earned it as a prize for my debut film. However, I never compromised on my shoes. I had two pairs, a sneaker with golden stripes and a high-rise puma shoe with multiple colors. They were my prized possessions and I cleaned them every week without fail. This ensured that they were always in the best condition and I could take pride in them.

I stepped out of the apartment, adjusted my messy hair, pushing it back away from my face. I ran my fingers through my beard, shaping it as I tossed my bag inside my car and headed to the bustling tea stall. This was a ritual I had grown accustomed to. The tea stall was always filled with familiar faces and the smell of freshly brewed tea and snacks made my mouth water. I lit my fourth cigarette that day and ordered my usual cup of tea.

My thoughts were occupied by smoke tendrils, distorted music playing in the background, and busy traffic. But suddenly, the stench of urine in that place brought back memories of the previous evening when I had been knocked off my feet, suddenly awakening to find a young girl hauntingly staring at me naked. Her eyes widened with horror, taking in the sight of my spread legs, covered in a light layer of sweat and pubic hair. I shuddered as the scene played over in my mind and felt an overwhelming wave of sadness. In that same place where I was having a regrettable goodnight's rest, two male dogs were aggressively making a mating call to a female dog. They ran around her, seemingly trying to win her attention.

A pang of regret enveloped me as I finished my tea and paid the bill. I had become a person unrecognizable even to myself, and an overpowering urge to elude this disappointment consumed me. I rushed out of the tea stall and headed for my car, hoping to outrun the sadness that had taken hold of me. I felt like a stranger in my own skin, and just wanted to get away. But no matter how fast I drove, I couldn't outrun the truth.

III

A grand opening of a new electronic store took place in the heart of Chennai city. The event was filled with excitement as the vibrant beats of Kerala music called chend melam echoed through the air. A troop of enthusiastic youngsters showcased their musical talent by playing energetic tunes on chenda drums at the entrance of the store. Their rhythmic beats captivated the attention of the passersby, drawing them towards the store.

The store's pamphlets were strategically displayed, enticing customers with unbelievable offers. These offers were not just meant to attract attention; they were designed to encourage people to step into the store and explore its wide range of mobile devices and accessories. The store promised a remarkable shopping experience, with a vast selection of cutting-edge smartphones, tablets, and other home appliances.

As customers entered the store, they were greeted by a modern and inviting ambiance. The spacious layout showcased the latest mobile technology, creating a sense of awe and curiosity among visitors. Knowledgeable staff members were ready to assist customers in finding the perfect mobile device that suited their needs and preferences. However, upon entering the store, potential buyers were informed that the offer only applied if they purchased a combo deal consisting of both a mobile phone and a smart watch. This clever sales tactic increased the overall purchase value and boosted profits. Furthermore, the store claimed to offer a wide range of washing machines. But their true intention was to sell a particular expensive washing machine that had been left unsold for an extended period. This particular machine had been transferred from another branch of their franchise, further indicating their desperation to sell it. Despite the shop's claims, many people entered purely for sightseeing purposes. They quickly discovered that the air cooler provided a welcome respite from the scorching afternoon heat. This allowed them to escape the oppressive weather and enjoy a brief relief. Additionally, the shop generously offered complimentary soft drinks to all visitors, further enhancing their experience.

Amidst the sea of people, the store manager emerged, clutching a sizable stash of five-hundred rupee notes. This roll of money appeared quite substantial, possibly amounting to ten to twenty thousand rupees in total. The crowd's attention immediately shifted to the manager. Their eyes filled with curiosity, wondering where he was headed with such a lot of money. He then called the three transgender individuals who were waiting for his arrival, and together they started walking towards him. Amongst the three, one of them was Simran. As they gathered around, Simran gracefully collected the money and blessed it with a heartfelt gaze. With the money in their possession, they moved away to find a quiet place where they could count it. The crowd, curious and intrigued, turned their attention towards Simran, eagerly waiting to see what she would do with the money.

Once Simran and her friends finished counting the money, Simran walked towards the entrance center. With confidence, she asked everyone to move to the side, creating a clear path for herself. Noticing Simran's actions, the manager joined in. With a professional tone, the manager addressed the customers, requesting them to wait for a while before crossing the entrance. She touched the money on her eyes again, an act of blessing, and put it in her mouth, balanced with her teeth. This ritual, rooted in tradition, held deep significance for her. It was believed to bring good fortune and ward off misfortune. After completing this initial step, she touched the floor, seeking another blessing. The floor, considered sacred ground, held powerful energies. By touching it, she hoped to connect with these energies and receive their divine blessings. Having received her blessing from the floor, she swiftly jumped, aiming to hit the top of the entrance door. The door, towering above her, represented new opportunities and possibilities. With a powerful leap, she stretched her body, extending her arm as far as she could, until her fingertips brushed against the top of the door. This ritual was not a one-time occurrence for her. Instead, she repeated it three to four times, reinforcing the blessings she sought. Each repetition deepened her connection to the divine, reaffirming her faith and commitment. Finally, after completing the rituals, they walked away from the store without looking back.

"Did you look at any other ads for rent?" Simran asked Sheela as they made their way back to their scooters.

"I tried talking to two owners today, but those bastards hung up after hearing my voice for a few seconds. Bastards!" She doubted that her manly voice, with its peculiar womanly tone, was the reason for it.

"Ok, but we have to find a place soon or else we will end up on the streets again. I heard they are bringing more girls next month," Simran said.

Sheela replied, "Yeah, yeah. And those girls must be beautiful. I heard they were young and would sell out easily. And they will throw us away and we will have no money. You saw this Lekha right? She is already in high demand for them. A rare piece they call her."

"She is a child, keep her away from this." Simran's face turned red with anger as the other two women couldn't help but burst into fits of giggles.

"A child with a beautiful body is good for business. Actually, if you are a woman and have a great cunt down there, you are good business. No matter how old you are. But you, you possess neither. So it is certain you are about to end up without money."

Simran clenched her fist tightly, her nails digging into her palms, as she tried to contain her rage. She punched Sheela on her back and said, "Shut your disgusting mouth and go check out that house Grace told about."

"Don't raise your hand on me. It hurts... And where are you going?"

"I saw this advertisement near this tea stall where we drank tea last night. Also, Lekha has been picked up by an early client. I will take her and check the house."

Sheela, imbued with obscene remarks added, "Only girls in high demand get clients during the day."

"I will see you at night." Simran scowled at them and started her scooter.

"Same street where we stood yesterday right?" Sheela screamed.

"Same street where we have been standing since last month." Simran screamed back as she drove away.

IV

I heard about the production house from a colleague and was intrigued by the opportunity they offered. As a writer, I always made sure I was up to date on any available opportunities in the industry, and this was certainly one I did not want to miss. After parking my car, I made my way to the production house to submit my work, or to discuss a story idea they had in mind.

Their office was located in a residential area. It was not very grand looking, but it had an old-fashioned charm. As I approached, I noticed a few young lads hanging around the garden. Inside the office, three more guys were sitting around an old wooden table, awaiting their turn. The walls were adorned with various antique paintings and photographs. There was a desk in the corner with books and paperwork scattered around it. A TV mounted at the top of the wall broadcast the live event of thousands of people marching joyfully in the streets, waving rainbow flags and proudly holding hands. The atmosphere was electric as the LGBTQ rally passed through the city. People of all ages, genders, and sexual orientations marched together, united in a common cause. The passion and energy was palpable as the crowd shouted chants of solidarity and celebration. Many people held signs saying "love is love" and "we are family". Smiles and laughter abounded as the crowd moved through the streets, united in their pride and joy.

The two guys next to me were in panic, their feet tapping against the floor and their eyes bulging with fear. I paid them no mind, instead turning away and taking out my draft from my bag. Although I felt their eyes on me, perhaps it was my age and grayed beard, so I ignored them. I ran my fingers over the dried ink on the paper. The delicate details I had so carefully crafted came to life at my touch. I found solace in my writing, even in the time of darkness. I reveled in the stories I wrote, even though I could never sell them. The draft was one of the stories I completed recently which talks about a judgmental society seen through the eyes of an innocent man. It is a world where people hate each other and give no love in return. It was a harsh and bitter reality, but I enjoyed bringing it to life.

A fiddle-footed man in his late 50's had a strange air of urgency about him as he quickly strode towards the office room. He stopped suddenly as he passed by me, giving me an unpleasant, piercing look through his rectangular framed glasses. My gaze shifted to his face as I noticed something peculiar—one of his thick gray mustache hairs had escaped its boundaries, curling outwards and touching his nostrils.

"Sir, why are you sitting here? Who let you in?" He asked me in a rushed, almost aggressive tone that instantly infuriated me. His words were clipped and hurried, as if he expected me to immediately understand the urgency of the situation.

"I came to meet the producer." I pointed my finger towards the office.

"Is the producer sir expecting your arrival?" He scrutinized me from head to toe as I stood there, searching for an answer. His stare was intense as he observed every inch of my being. I could feel his eyes absorbing every detail.

"No. I came to know that your production house is looking for a writer and I want to submit my script."

"The stories of the people waiting here have been shortlisted and awaiting final confirmation from the boss. You may place your manuscript or whatever you have at that table and we will contact you. You are not allowed to be here without an invitation." He looked me in the eyes as he tried to grab my hands in the middle of the sentence.

"I am no debut writer and my story was once made into a successful movie."

"Everyone here holds that badge of yours. Now please leave the place."

I scowled at the three guys, my nerves betraying me. I retorted, "You don't compare me to these kids. What do you write?... Your failed romance or a remake of a movie you watched last week?... Or those stupid films with irrelevant songs and dance?"

I yelled at the top of my lungs, pushing him away from me with all my might. He stumbled back, surprised and taken aback by my sudden outburst. I glared at him, not wanting him to come close.

"Sir, keep your voice down and leave the place." He put his hands up in the air, a sign of surrender, and said in a firm voice.

The guys waiting in the queue looked at me anxiously, their eyes full of anticipation. I could feel the tension in the air, and suddenly, a lean woman came out of the office room. Glancing around the room, she observed the scene before closing the door quietly.

"Sir, you need to leave now." The man whispered again.

As the years went by, rejection and humiliation became familiar companions in my life. With another load of disappointment and defeat weighing down on my shoulders, I turned away from yet another failed attempt. The scrutiny of judgmental eyes bore into me as I strode away with purpose. Hastily, I returned my draft to my bag and pushed away the guy approaching me at the entrance.

On my way to the office, I parked my car in front of a wine shop and rushed inside, pushing through the throng of people. I shouted for the cheapest bottle of whisky that cost a hundred rupees. The money slipped from my fingers as the bottle was placed in my palm. I fought my way through the crowd, tightly gripping the whisky bottle in my hand. A petty store at the entrance to the wine shop allowed me to buy a Pepsi bottle. I poured the bottle content onto the ground, filled the bottle with whisky, took a swig and started the engine.

V

When it was over, the man was disappointed that he came within seconds after several minutes of foreplay. Lekha tried to push him away saying he had just paid for a shot. However, he continued to hump on her, his hands tightly holding her round breast as he sucked her shoulders. After a while, he was irritated by her whining and choked her saying, "You fucking think you can control me?... Are you that strong?... Are you a strong girl now?"

Lekha screamed out of her strength, seeking help, but he shoved his fingers inside her mouth as he dragged her to the floor. The man then stretched her mouth and forced her to blow until she was choked to death. And when he could not hear more of her whimpering, he dragged her by her hair, opened the door and throwed her at the entrance.

To put on his pants, he walked inside naked. The room was dimly lit, and Lekha was lying at the entrance, her breast hanging out. Swiftly, she pulled her blouse back into place and wiped her mouth. Spying his slipper by the doorway, she hurled it directly at his face. Enraged, the man's tolerance reached its limit, propelling him toward her with intent to harm once more. Summoning all her strength, she fled the room, draping her saree as she went.

From the balcony of the motel, the man lecherously eyed her, while Lekha, meeting his gaze head-on, brushed away her tears, secured her hair, and cast a curse by flinging sand into the air. This was something she had learned from Simran.

Simran stood patiently on the opposite side of the road. As soon as she spotted Lekha's mascara smudging across her face, she inquired about what had happened. But Lekha maintained a stoic silence, urging Simran to move quickly.

As they continued on their way, Simran persisted in questioning Lekha, desperate to understand the cause of her distress. She ranted about a man who was evidently pressuring her into finding clients during the daytime. Simran's frustration and concern were palpable, but Lekha remained resolutely silent, desperately attempting to regain control over her teary emotions. The weight of the unspoken words hung heavy between them. Each step they took further emphasized Lekha's emotional turmoil. Simran continued to support her through persistent questioning and empathetic rants.

Simran informed Lekha that she needed to visit a few houses before dropping Lekha back in her own room. Upon hearing this, Lekha remained silent, yet Simran deciphered the meaning behind her silence. This unspoken communication was common between the two friends, who had developed a deep bond of understanding and familiarity.

Simran's first house was a complete disaster, much like all the other houses she had inquired about in the past few days. Upon reaching the house, Simran rang the bell, and an elderly man cautiously opened the door partially, responding to her from the entrance. A door, a small porch, and a locked grill gate separated Simran and the house owner, creating considerable distance between them. As a result, Simran had no choice but to raise her voice to communicate with the elderly man. She claimed to be the one who made the phone call and said she had come to see the house. The man observed them for a moment, contemplating their presence. After a brief pause, he gestured with his hand, indicating they should leave. He entered the house in a relaxed manner.

Simran, known for her fiery temper, unleashed a torrent of angry words at him, just as she always does. Frustrated and desperate to vent her anger physically, she began searching frantically for something to throw at his house. However, to her dismay, there was nothing within her reach that could serve her purpose. Realizing the futility of her search, Lekha swiftly intervened and forcefully pulled Simran out of that place. Lekha, understanding the need to calm her friend's frayed nerves, tried her best to soothe Simran's anger and restore her composure.

After their visit to the first house, they proceeded to visit another house in the evening. Simran dialed the number of the person who had posted the ad for the second house. The phone rang, and to Simran's surprise, a young man in his early twenties was waiting just across the street. As soon as their eyes met, the guy seemed to panic, his expression filled with fear or apprehension.

"Can we see the house?" Simran walked towards the gate. Despite her persistent movement, the man standing near the house remained motionless.

He then said the house has already been booked by another party.

"Then why are you waiting here for us?" Simran's anger boiled over as she saw the guy retreat. Her frustration, pent up for so long, surged forward like a raging river. And with each step he took backwards.

"I was waiting to inform you."

Simran, consumed by unbridled anger and frustration, could no longer keep her emotions in check. In her heightened state of agitation, she noticed a pile of stones conveniently located nearby. Without hesitation, she instinctively gathered a handful of stones in her trembling hands. With each stone firmly gripped, she hurled them towards the man who was the target of her ire. Her actions were fueled by blind rage, and each stone served as a physical manifestation of her pent-up anger and resentment. The stones flew through the air, propelled by her fury, as she aimed them with precision and intensity.

"You bastards will rot in hell. I will one day make you all burn while I shine a castle. Rot in hell... bastards!"

Lekha's attempt to pull her proved futile as Simran's strength surpassed hers. Sensing the need to intervene, the people nearby protected the boy, shielding him from harm. As the crowd united in their efforts, their collective energy fueled a pursuit to drive Simran away. They chased after her, determined to keep the boy safe. Simran, realizing she had no other options left, reluctantly left the place.

Together, Lekha and Simran hopped into their vehicle and flew away from the scene. However, Simran's anger and frustration continued to manifest as she ranted, her words echoing in the air as they distanced themselves from the situation.

"I would have killed them all with stones if you were not with me... God, you saved those bastards from my rage... I should have killed them."

She stopped abruptly at the corner of the street, her breath quickening as she glanced back at the sea of faces that had caused her distress. Anger surged through her veins, and with a venomous glare, she loudly cursed them one last time before escaping from the scene.

***

Simran and Lekha had discovered a hidden gem in the city — a favorite place to escape the chaos of everyday life. Nestled amidst the mountains, this serene hilltop offered breathtaking views of the entire city. From their homes, it took them only a short drive and a long walk to get there.

Simran, always attuned to Lekha's emotions, noticed that her friend was still carrying the weight of worry on her shoulders. Determined to help her find solace, Simran suggested they visit their cherished spot on the hilltop. She believed that the sweeping vistas and the natural beauty would provide the perfect environment for Lekha to let go of her stress and worries.

The air was crisp and the gentle breeze rustled the surrounding trees' leaves. Simran could see the tension in Lekha's face melt away as they stood there, taking in the panoramic view of the sprawling city below. The twinkling lights and distant sounds of the city seemed distant and insignificant from this vantage point. To their right lay the airport runway, another vantage point from which they could witness flights landing and taking off at regular intervals. As Lekha observed these aircraft, her mind would delve deep into contemplation, a multitude of questions amassing within her chest for which she had no answers.

They found a comfortable spot on a rock and sat in silence, both lost in their thoughts. As they sat there, time seemed to stand still. Simran could feel Lekha gradually relaxing, her worries fading into the background. They didn't need to say a word; their presence and the shared experience of being in this tranquil place spoke volumes.

"Do not look at me, I am about to remove my wig." Said Simran.

Simran and Lekha shared the same room and became accustomed to this arrangement. Simran disliked seeing her own face whenever she removed her wig. To avoid this discomfort, she asked Lekha to turn around while removing it. Although Lekha always obliged, they both knew that Lekha secretly enjoyed watching Simran at this moment.

Simran, feeling the heat on her bald head, decided to cool off by splashing some water onto her scalp. She gently rubbed her head, wiping away the sweat that had accumulated. After refreshing herself, she reached for her wig and carefully placed it back on her head, ensuring it fit snugly.

Taking a seat next to Lekha, Simran retrieved the fresh mango juice they had purchased earlier. Pouring it into a paper cup, she handed it to Lekha, who accepted the refreshing drink with a smile. As Lekha took a sip, Simran noticed there was still some juice left in the foil cover. Without hesitation, she drank the remaining juice, not letting any go to waste.

"Do you believe in hope?" Lekha asked.

"What is hope?" Simran looked perplexed. The question seemed to be inappropriate given the situation for her.

"It is something... like... you wish for it, though it is far away from your reach. Yet you still believe you could acquire it someday," Lekha explained, and she blushed, looking at Simran's confused expression.

"No... I try not to think much about life. It is easy to live that way. Today is good. Tomorrow could be a surprise... Why are you asking? What do you hope for?" As Simran looked into Lekha's eyes, she was enchanted by the sunset reflection within them.

"If there was no hope, I would have killed myself when those bastards lay over me to satisfy their needs. Everyone hopes for something, I guess. Religious people pray to God, which is an act of hope; daydreaming when you are at work about something significant is also an act of hope. Working hard every day and continuing with it is also a hope that you wish your life would change someday. I believe hope is something we all have in common as humans."

"Oh, that's very dangerous. I hoped for so many things as a kid. And then when I grew up, I realized life is about 90% of things you don't get that you wish for, 5% of things you get you have wished for, and the remaining 5% are things you receive out of surprise. I still find life to be beautiful. You know why?"

Lekha nodded her head, and Simran whispered, "Because... I really don't give a shit. And now, everything looks beautiful around me."

"So, you say you don't wish for anything? You don't wish to get out of this dump called life?" Lekha's face turned into a big wrinkle.

After thinking for a while, Simran replied, "Maybe, I do hope for something. When we were kids, my brother and I would always sit outside our house. Our house was a small area that encompassed a bedroom, a kitchen, and a living space at each corner, all within a single unified space. So, I would take my brother outside, and we would eat there, study there, play, and also sleep outside at night. Sometimes at night, I would find it difficult to sleep, so I would gaze at the huge sky lying there on the ground and watch the stars twinkle. Since then, I have always been mesmerized by the stars and their relationship with the sky. When I am sad, I would look at the sky; when I am happy, I would look at the sky. And... someday, I wish I could have my own tiny house and a place from where I can lay and talk to the stars in the sky. Yeah, I hope for this." Simran appeared both surprised and excited as she unraveled a thought that had resided within her, yet remained concealed even from her own awareness.

"How old are you?" Lekha interrupted her.

Simran quickly turned to her, coming out from her trance-like state, and said, "You are not supposed to ask a woman about her age."

Lekha laughed and said, "But I am sure you must have crossed your twenties. So... what would you say to a 20-year-old when she seeks life advice from you? I am in my twenties, so what are the mistakes I am not supposed to make?"

“I don’t know... maybe make enough mistakes... or do not take any advice." Simran was unsure of what to say, desperately searching for the right words to express herself.

When Lekha asked why not to take advice, Simran replied, "They all lecture you about the shit they’ve been through. But you have to experience your own life. Embrace the adventure that awaits you. Do not follow the path explored and ruined.”

“But one thing about life that you would like to tell yourself?”

“Life is ugly. But we can make it beautiful. And everything that is to do with our past is about to become a story someday. So I think we should make it a worthy story. Also, hope would kill me... so I would tell myself, I don’t know... kill hope? But that would be incorrect advice. See that’s why I don’t give or take any advice."

“But hope keeps me alive and I cannot think of a life without hope.” Lekha stood up.

“Yes, good for you. Keep your hopes high. Because I have a gift for you and you will find it tomorrow." Said Simran as she ran ahead of Lekha, her excitement palpable.

"What’s this gift?" Lekha paused and wondered.

"It’s a surprise, so you’ll see it when you see it. Now keep moving, I have to leave, I am late.”

Simran, devoid of patience, chose not to wait for Lekha and instead proceeded to descend the staircase with haste. Meanwhile, Lekha’s mind was occupied with thoughts of the gift she had been contemplating. Realizing that Simran had no intention of waiting, Lekha decided to follow her, driven by curiosity.

VI

I watched through my car windshield as people strolled in and out of the office building, dressed in fancy clothing and sharing laughter. I had just finished the last mouthful of whisky from my bottle and was smoking my 11th cigarette of the day. Seeing these people brought up a swirl of questions—was their joy real, or were they putting on a show? Could I ever be as genuinely happy as them, or be as good at pretending? I stared out of the window, unsure and lost in thought.

For those few seconds in the office elevator, it felt like an eternity. I stood out like a sore thumb among the neat and tidy earbuds in the see-through container. All the other earbuds were gleaming white, while I was a dingy brown. The air was so thick and heavy that it was difficult to breathe. The overpowering scent of the various perfumes and colognes of the people around me was almost too much for my nose. I had to fight to hold back a sneeze. On top of that, the office was located on the seventh floor, and with the amount of whisky I had consumed, I was sure I would stumble and fall in the middle of the ride.

Working for a magazine company was far from ideal. However, it was an easy job and I needed the money to support my habit of smoking cigarettes, drinking alcohol, and eating one meal a day. The majority of the stories in the magazine were related to politics, but my department, the movie and book reviews, only filled a small column in the publication. As a result, the job was not the most fulfilling, but it was necessary to help me get by. Movies have always been a source of entertainment, but for me, they have become mundane and dull. I can't help but think that the era of truly remarkable films is a thing of the past. Most magazines simply cover movies surrounded by controversy or commercial cinema. When I had to review a movie, I would wander around and get some perspective from people who had seen the movie and fill my write-up with interesting and meaningful quotes, which the company liked.

My job wasn't the most enjoyable experience, but it helped me stick to my writing habit. Even though I wasn't particularly enthusiastic about the topics I wrote about, I enjoyed the process of putting words together and creating something meaningful. Those few hours I spent writing every day were a great way to focus my energy on something. But I hated the monotony of sitting in those cubicles, surrounded by my co-workers‘ constant buzzing. The work was not particularly demanding and the salary was not very high, so I often felt I could come and leave as I pleased. I was often late for work, or wouldn't show up at all, and at times I would be so drunk that the security guards would have to wake me up and ask me to leave.

I walked through the office hallway, as others walked out to take a lunch break. Suddenly, I heard someone calling my name. I turned around and saw the HR person waving at me from her cabin. She motioned for me to come in, and I stepped into her office. It was clear that she wanted to talk to me about something, so I braced myself and waited for her to speak.

She had a habit of wearing snug attire that revealed her cleavage, and she was skimming through some documents when my attention was inadvertently drawn to it. I hadn't meant to focus on her cleavage, but the haze induced by alcohol led me to gaze at it momentarily. To my astonishment, she raised her eyes and inquired if I needed water. Caught in the act, I felt a surge of embarrassment, yet I graciously declined her offer.

A shiver coursed down my spine as I confronted the impending reality. This scenario felt all too familiar – a pattern I had witnessed when individuals were let go from the company. The room exuded a somber atmosphere, with only the ticking of the clock reverberating through the air. I gazed at the table, fixating on the documents sprawled across it, half-expecting her to broach the subject. I resolved not to complicate matters, opting to swiftly address the heart of the situation. I did not want to skirt around the issue or waste any time. Instead, I came straight to the point and laid out the facts.

"Do you want me to quit?" I looked into her eyes.

After thinking for a few seconds, she cleared her throat and said, "Yes. Management thinks it's right for the company and you know why." She seemed to be scared of me when I stepped closer to her. Her expression shifted from confusion to fear, and her body language changed as she stepped back.

I stared at my reflection in the window glass behind her, my appearance unkempt. My eyes were sunken, my lips parched, and my shirt clung to me with sweat. Despite working two years at this job, I couldn't help but ponder the uncertainties that would envelop me if it were suddenly taken away. Six months' rent loomed over me, and I had already sold all of my possessions to survive. A sense of hopelessness engulfed, leaving me feeling isolated, with an uncertain future ahead. Without uttering a word, I rose to my feet and exited the premises, adjusting my bag over my shoulder.

***

Exiting through the automatic glass door, my frustration surged towards the fan that had been broken the previous night. I had depended on it, and yet it had proven futile in saving my life for nothing. Consumed by anger, I ignited a cigarette, and strangely, it was an oddly personal encounter; my emotions mirrored those I would feel when angered by an individual. "Damn it you bloody three-legged pathetic machine. I will smash you into pieces." I vowed.

At that same moment I saw the rich young boy step out of his Porsche Panamera. I was instantly filled with disdain. He had a smooth complexion, which told me he was probably no older than eighteen or nineteen. At the peak of summer, he wore a heavy coat, a sure sign of his privileged upbringing. I despised these rich kids who had been given advantages that others could only dream of; they had no talent, no ambition, and lived off their families' wealth.

The tendrils of smoke from my cigarette trailed in the air and I couldn't look away as he walked into the restaurant. He waved off the smoke from my cigarette, and when he accidentally tapped my shoulder, his stare lingered for a few seconds. I was transfixed, but he eventually broke away and entered. I continued to stand there, watching him become swallowed up by the darkness of the restaurant.

I took a deep breath and exhaled as I walked towards my car. The fear of the unknown engulfed me. I felt like a complete failure, and I was so far from improving my life. I knew I couldn't be like everyone else, or pretend to be happy like them. It felt like I would never write a good story again, and I was getting older. I clenched my fist and jaw tightly after dropping my cigarette, feeling even more hopeless than before.

My world felt like it was crashing down around me, and I had no idea how to fix it. I felt stuck in this never-ending cycle of despair and powerlessness to do anything. I took a few more steps towards my car and kept walking. I quickly spun around as I sensed a sudden surge of adrenaline and the urge to take out all my anger on someone. The spoiled rich kid in the restaurant seemed like the most appropriate target for my wrath. My fists were clenched in anticipation and was ready to release the fury building up inside me.

I took heavy steps and walked inside the restaurant, taking in the sudden change in ambience. Soft jazz played in the distance, and waiters walked between the tables, taking orders and delivering food. I scanned around the place for a moment before spotting the kid at a corner table, laughing and chatting with three young girls. The kid's cheerful mood was infectious, and I couldn't help but lighten. I walked towards him. His look was intense and unwavering, and the laughter that had filled the room only moments before evaporated. I placed my fists on the table in front of him, my knuckles turning white from the pressure. His eyes glared at me, and I knew he was not happy with the situation.

"Didn't your papa teach you how to say sorry?"

He stared at me with food in his mouth, his eyes wide open in confusion. He nodded slowly, as if trying to make sense of the situation. His expression was disbelief, and I could tell he had no idea what was going on. I could feel my own confusion, and I knew that he was just as perplexed as I was.

But I disliked his scowl, or I looked for a reason. I slowly stepped behind him, my hands encircling his tiny head. With one powerful swoop, I slammed his face onto the plate. Food scattered around us, on the walls and on the floor. His eyes widened in shock, while the girls screamed in terror. Bracing his head again, I slammed it onto the table with all my might. His nose bled profusely and his teeth flew out of his mouth. I pulled the boy by the neck and threw him to the floor with a thud. He was so weak that he rolled onto the opposite table. A security guard approached me quickly, but I was prepared. I delivered a swift punch with my fist, knocking him off his feet. Not wanting to take any chances, I stretched my leg to the chest of the other security guard who followed him, and laid him off too.

The boy trembled as I approached him. He covered his face with both hands, and I could see blood dripping from his fingers. I found a comfortable position to sit on his thin waist. His wrist was so slender that I could easily pull it off with just one hand. Taking my glasses off the floor, I adjusted my hair to fall to the side. As I put them back on, I could already feel the power of the situation, and the control I had over the boy. I felt my hand come down hard on his face and heard his cries of fear and pain. I felt no remorse or guilt as I searched for answers in my life, for the mess I had become. The boy kept screaming and crying until four to five security guards and waiters pulled me off him and walked me out of the restaurant.

For a moment, I saw myself in that boy and wanted to let out all the anger I had about what I had turned into.

Every punch I threw felt like I was trying to rip my own face apart, eventually I became weak. The guards held me so tight that I could barely move, and I had become numb and tired of life. Through the glass window, I saw a little girl sitting atop the high raised wooden chair, her legs dangling off the edge and staring at me. I adjusted my glasses, which had slipped down my nose, and straightened my shirt. She had a beautiful headband that looked like a delicate crown gathered with soft, colorful flowers. She looked like a princess. Her innocent frown reflected my guilt. I felt a sense of shame, her look burning into my back.

Suddenly, I was taken aback when I sensed a warm touch on my wrist. This tightened its grip as it pushed the guard behind me into the bush. I felt the grip on my bones and turned my head to see a transwoman. She grabbed my hand and ran towards my car, screaming and wheezing at the same time. "Run... run... go away you bastards!" She shouted those words until we reached my car.

I was startled when I got into the car and saw Simran, the transwoman I had been seeking pleasure in to satisfy my lust. She was sitting there, her face only inches away from mine, and her words were loud and clear. "Drive, you fucking idiot!" she yelled. I could feel the heat of her breath on my skin, and I knew I had to get us out of there. I started the engine and drove away, my heart pounding as one of the security guards tried to get into the car window and grab my shoulders, preventing me from driving off. He was determined to call the police but Simran intervened, scrambling between me and the steering, punching the guard hard. I could barely see the road ahead or maintain control of the steering. The road appeared hazy, with Simran's hair obscuring my view as she lay across my arms. She bit the guard's hand, delivering punches to his face relentlessly, displaying every ounce of aggression in her attempt to force him to release his grip and flee from the car. The guard hung onto the window until we reached the main road, but eventually let go and gave up.

Simran's face was contorted with rage as she looked me in the eye. Without warning, she pulled her arm back and slapped me hard across the face. Her voice was loud and full of anger as she shouted "You dumb drunk bastard!"

VII

Apu felt relieved to have finally found a parking spot two streets away from his house. As he walked into his home, he noticed splashes of mud on his calf. Wearing shorts on a rainy evening turned out to be a mistake. He quickly walked to the bathroom to shower, and the warm water provided much-needed relief for his tired body.

Feeling refreshed, Apu decided to stretch his muscles to ease the tension. Then, he reached for his shoulder bag to grab the dinner packed by Bejoy, his manager. Having often worked late and not having time to prepare a meal, Apu blushed at Bejoy's thoughtfulness. The food was heated and served at the dining table. Taking a seat, he felt a sense of anticipation for the meal ahead. However, as he looked around, he couldn't shake off the unease that settled in the air. The room seemed unusually quiet, devoid of any sound except for his own breathing. It was as if silence itself had suffocated him.

Behind the house, there was a graveyard, and the thought sent shivers down his spine, amplifying his anxiety. The stillness of the room only magnified the haunting presence of the graveyard. Lost in his thoughts, he continued to eat. The crunching sound of his chewing seemed impossibly loud in the overwhelming quietness of the room. For the first time, he became acutely aware of every morsel he consumed, the sound resonating in his ears.

Just as he was beginning to adjust to the eerie atmosphere, his phone rang, shattering the silence. Startled, he reached for his phone and saw the contact name displayed on the screen, Maya. Curiosity mingled with apprehension as he wondered why she was calling him at this moment.

When he picked up the phone, he could hardly contain his excitement. "Hi Maya, have you reached home?"

"Yes, sir. I just did. It's raining heavily here. What about there?"

"No, I could only hear sounds of thunder occasionally," Apu replied, the excitement evident in his voice.

Maya couldn't help but tease, "Are you getting used to your stay, or are you still hallucinating noises from the burial ground behind you?" She left out a mocking smile.

Apu chuckled nervously. "Oh, I am glad you called, but let's not talk about it." As he glanced around the old ancestral house, the silence and the orange glow of his residence gave him an inexplicable haunting experience.

Maya had called to ask for some details. "Umm... we are having this board printed for the play, and Bejoy wanted me to collect some of your details for registration purposes."

"Ok, but I saw the design, and, to be honest, I didn't like it. It's kind of... umm... How to say, like giving the audience a different perspective. I think you should make it more blue than red," Apu suggested.

"Yeah, I thought exactly the same. But we are running late, and the show is in 3 days, so we cannot change it now," Maya sighed.

Apu balanced his mobile between his ear and shoulders as he walked into the kitchen to wash his dishes. "Ok, tell me the details you need. But we could have done this at the theater. We were there all day."

"Yeah, I know. But I am 19 and irresponsible. Teenage... you know, please bear with me. Let me grab your form. Give me a minute." Maya searched for the registration form and looked for Apu's name on it.

"Let's do this. Your full name? That is a stupid question; it's already written,"

Apu smiled and got back to the dining table.

"Age?"

"42"

"You don't look like you are 42, but still I have to write it down."

"That is so modest of you even after seeing my beard turn gray and hair balding."

They continued with the registration process. As Maya asked questions about his relationship status, residential details, and his experience.

Before ending the call, she made sure to reconfirm the details of their earlier discussion that day. "You're surely going to join me in this pride rally right? I am sure you will be fascinated and your presence will be so helpful."

Apu's playful giggle resonated through the phone as he responded, "Of course, I will join you. But let's make sure we both return to the theater on time; we have to get ready for our play."

Maya smiled at Apu's enthusiasm. "Absolutely," she agreed wholeheartedly. "We'll make it back in time for the play, no worries."

With the plan confirmed, they bid each other goodnight, a sense of excitement and camaraderie lingering in the air as they ended the call.

As Maya's voice faded from the other end of the line, Apu sat alone at the dining table, the weight of the conversation settling in his chest. Memories from Apu's past began to resurface. He stared at the wall, trying to block these memories that threatened to consume him. But like a relentless tide, they came rushing back, memories of a time when he was an artist, a master of expression and emotion.

Back in his homeland, the place he had left two decades ago, Apu found himself grappling with memories that he had once believed he could suppress. Returning to the familiar surroundings of Thrissur, a city in Kerala, even if only for a week, proved to be a journey into the depths of his past. His attempts to control those thoughts failed miserably. Every street he walked down, every corner he turned, held a piece of his history. The nostalgia that enveloped him was both comforting and overwhelming. Faces from the past seemed to emerge from the shadows, haunting him with their presence. Each encounter brought with it a flood of emotions, a kaleidoscope of joy, regret, and longing.

His mind drifted to that fateful night when he stood on the stage as a Kathakali artist, his face adorned with vibrant colors that symbolized characters from ancient epics. The applause had been thunderous, a symphony of appreciation for the art he poured his heart and soul into. The connection he felt with the audience was unparalleled, as if he was a conduit for the stories of his ancestors, passed down through generations. As he closed his eyes, the scent of the paint on his face seemed to waft through the air, transporting him back in time. He could feel the fabric of his traditional costume against his skin, the weight of responsibility as he portrayed characters with a depth of emotion that moved even the hardest hearts. The music of the chenda and mizhavu drums resonated in his ears, enveloping him in a trance-like state.

But life had taken him on a different path. The allure of the silver screen had beckoned, and he had embraced the world of cinema. Success had followed, and he had become a celebrated film star, adored by millions. Yet, deep down, he felt like a wanderer in a foreign land, yearning for the familiar embrace of his cultural roots. Apu's heart ached with a poignant mix of nostalgia and regret. He had sacrificed his true passion for the allure of fame and fortune. In the process, he had lost a part of himself—the artist who once danced with the gods, creating magic on the stage.

In the stillness of that moment, as the echoes of his past reverberated within him, Apu made a solemn vow which he would tell to himself every night for the past three years—"I will fix my life."

VIII

Simran named herself after a famous Indian actress in tribute to her beauty. She had a rough and coarse voice that was often heard echoing through the walls. Her face was always adorned with a healthy pink blush of makeup and she had an exquisite sense of style dominated by glittering silk sarees that accentuated her thick waist. Her wrists were always covered with plastic bangles that made a delightful clinking sound every time she walked into a room.

I lay my back down on the floor, propped my legs up on the bed and rested my head on my arms. Simran quickly moved around the house, trying to open all the windows and let in any breeze. The fan was broken and put aside, leaving us to swelter in 38 degree heat that burned our skin. She talked to herself, ranting about everyone and everything. It was a habit she had; she always did it. Then, suddenly, her attention shifted towards me. She sat down close to my face and grabbed my hand, tenderly wiping away the blood that had collected there. Her movements were gentle, almost soothing, as she cleaned away the evidence of whatever had happened. Her actions and soft words comforted me strangely.

"Why did you hit him? Do you know the boy?"

I smirked and said "How do you expect me to know a boy who is 18 and drives such an expensive car?"

When she finished wiping the blood from my fingernails, out of habit, she loosen the drawstrings of my pajamas. I immediately stopped her, not wanting her to go further.

She felt a deep sense of humiliation as she kicked my waist and stood up. Her gaze then fell to the floor, where my shoes lay. Scanning them, she noticed the words "Fuck" on the left shoe and "You" on the right shoe, both embroidered or inked on the sole. Her eyes widened with amazement and curiosity as she opened the sack where I kept all my old shoes. To her surprise, the pattern was the same. She giggled as she ran her fingers over each character.

"You walk around the streets wearing these shoes? Why do you have this printed on all of them?" She couldn't contain her excitement as it bubbled up inside her, and before she knew it, she laughed from deep within her stomach.

I couldn't take my eyes off the broken fan pipe hanging from the ceiling, surrounded by a mess of wires. The ceiling was damp from water, and the cement was turning a sickly green color, and its texture had become rough. It felt like a symbol of my life, in shambles. I stayed there for a while, lost in my thoughts, staring at the ceiling until I finally snapped out of it.

"My mother used to tell us stories when we were kids that people of our caste were not allowed to wear footwear. We were abused, beaten and molested for putting on one. I decided then that when I grow up I will wear shoes of different colors and curse all those privileged bastards with pride."

Simran wandered through my room, scanning my other possessions, and paying particular attention to the watch. She commented that she had seen similar, more expensive watches on her clients. Then, she picked up one of my awards from the shelf. I didn't appreciate her prying into my life and getting too personal. I spoke up weakly, without energy, but sternly told her to put the award back. She scrutinized every item in my possession without uttering a word—my awards, stack of drafts, wardrobe, and all that occupied that lifeless space. Then, she leaped onto my bed, and I extended my legs to the floor, stretching myself out.

"Are you rich?" She asked, her eyes fixed on the same portion of the ceiling where mine had been. Her contemplation was equally intense, as if she were attempting to see through the white plaster above us.

"I am a writer." I replied, expressionless.

Her question instantly brought me back to my past. For a few seconds, it felt like a nightmare. Memories of the darkness and despair that had plagued me for so long flooded my mind. I was filled with dread. A memory where I felt broken as I walked through the empty street, tears streaming down my face as I remembered the events that had transpired. Just twenty six years ago, my family tried to marry me off to a 14-year-old girl, something I refused. They tried to convince me that my dreams of a career in cinema were a sin. Instead, I should conform to societal norms and values forced upon us in the name of culture and religion.

And so, I ran away from my village, sobbing and wheezing, striving to make a life for myself and follow my dreams. I knew it would be difficult, but I was determined to break free from the shackles of my family and society and create a life of my own. I was ready to face whatever challenges came my way and build a future for myself. The day I decided I wanted a different life was the day my war against myself began. Two decades later, I felt like I had ended up doing things that I had always tried to run away from.

"What is life like for you?" she asked her next question.

"Have you ever thought about killing yourself?"

I didn't feel like answering her, so I dodged it and shot back a completely inappropriate question. I slowly raised myself from the floor and brought my legs close to my chest to rest my back against the bed.

"We all do. In this cruel world, everyone thinks about killing himself. But we don't have the courage to do it."

Her legs dangled over my side. We both sat mesmerized by the sight of the clear blue sky through the square-shaped window. It seemed like a framed painting, almost as if we were looking at it from a museum. I couldn't take my eyes off it, and I could tell she felt the same. The sky seemed to stretch on forever, and I zoned out to that serene moment, feeling peace and calm wash over me. The tranquility engulfed me, making me feel like we were the only ones in this world.

I could feel the rough texture of Simran's saree on my shoulders, and it was like a wave of nostalgia. I was again taken back to the days when I lay on my mother's lap, and she caressed me with her tender love. Thinking about that moment, I slowly leaned my head onto Simran's lap and was surprised to feel her gently stroking my hair and beard. A single tear trickled down my temple, as I was overwhelmed by pure emotion in that moment.

"What if you get a chance to end your life? Will you do it?" I broke the silence between us.

After thinking for a while, she said, "No, I have reached a point where I only see the beautiful occurrences of this universe. Have you ever gazed at the night sky? When you stretch your neck and gaze at the sky, you face several questions. As a response, a few stars may flicker. You are captivated by how abundant this universe is. Is there life on those stars? In the night, does someone stretch their neck and think of me at any of those stars just like I do from here? Will we see anyone from other planets? If so, have you imagined how they would look? Or what if there was a universe that accepts someone like me? A man who loves to experience a woman's body but must sell it to survive in this cruel world?"

She gracefully extended her arms, reaching towards the heavens, inviting the sky and all its beauty to come to her. She waved her hands rhythmically, her movements like a dance, as if she wanted to capture the sky in her hands. And she said, "However, in the end, I think we're just a tiny drama in this massive space."

"But how can life be meaningful if you fail at what you are passionate about? What is life if you don't get to live with the person you love? What is life when you lose control of yourself and become a foreigner in your own soul? And what is life if there is no hope?"

The words poured out of me as another evening sun broke through the horizon, its orange rays spilling into our room with warmth and light. I pressed my cheek gently against her knees and rubbed the tears flowing down my face. We stayed there in silence, the air between us thickening. I lay on her lap, her hands dancing to some unheard hum, her other hand gently caressing me like I was still a child. I could feel the warmth radiating from her hands, a comfort and assurance I needed in that moment. Life felt peaceful and safe, a stillness in the midst of chaos. I closed my eyes and let silence and her touch embrace me. In this tiny room with everything nature could offer, we were two broken souls seeking solace.

IX

Apu woke up the next morning to the gentle chime of his phone, signaling an incoming video call. With a sleepy yawn, he answered the call, and to his delight, his daughter's face filled the screen. Her bright eyes and infectious smile instantly warmed his heart, making it feel as though she had filled his entire day with sunshine.

"Hi, papa one!" Ruhi's sweet voice rang through the phone.

"Hello, my little princess!" Apu replied, his face lighting up with joy. He blew a kiss to the mobile screen, and Ruhi giggled, returning the gesture.

Their conversation was a dance of love and affection, even though the words between them were few. They expressed their feelings through waves, kisses, and laughter. It was a language only they understood, a silent bond that transcended the limitations of speech.

Ruhi then shyly confessed to Apu, "Papa one, I had an accident last night. I peed on the bed, and papa two had to clean it up. He didn't get much sleep, and I felt bad for ruining his rest."

Farhaan, who was standing behind Ruhi, lovingly hugged her and left a long kiss on her cheek. Apu smiled at the sight of their affectionate bond, grateful for the beautiful family he had found.

Ruhi had come into their lives when she was just five years old, and Apu and Farhaan had been married for three years at that time. They had made the decision to adopt Ruhi, and she had quickly become the center of their universe.

To Ruhi, Apu was 'papa one' and Farhaan was 'papa two'. It had happened quite naturally. When they first brought her home, she had asked them how she should address them. Farhaan suggested she call them both by their names, but Ruhi had respectfully disagreed, saying that elders should not be called by their names. So, Apu suggested she call him "papa one" and Farhaan "papa two." Farhaan had playfully pretended to be jealous of Apu being called number one and him being number two, but they had embraced the endearing titles ever since.

"Okay, my little angel, it's time for school now. Say bye to papa one," Farhaan gently reminded Ruhi.

Apo and Ruhi waved at each other again, showering virtual kisses on the mobile screen.

"Who is taking her to school?" Apu asked.

"Rani amma is a great help here, as I am so occupied with my work," Farhaan explained.

"And who is Rani amma?" Apu inquired, surprised that he hadn't heard of her before.

"I told you that I had to find an alternative for Sunitha to take care of Ruhi while she is gone to her native place. So, she brought Rani amma home, and she and Ruhi are getting along really well," Farhaan replied, a soft smile playing on his lips.

"I'm glad Ruhi is comfortable with her," Apu said, pleased that Ruhi was adapting to the new arrangement.

Farhaan paused for a moment before adding, "She gets along easily with everyone, doesn't she? She is so lovely."

Apu nodded, appreciating Ruhi's ability to form bonds effortlessly. He asked Farhaan to hold on for a moment as he splashed some water on his face. The morning light filtered through the window, casting a warm glow on his features. The conversation lightened. Apu brushed his teeth, made his morning coffee, and did his yoga routine, all while still on the call. On the other side, Farhaan had already started his day, finished his coffee, done an online yoga session with his peers, and was checking his emails every now and then. Farhaan worked for a Tech Giant E-Commerce company as a Business Analyst. Even though Apu had little knowledge and interest in the intricacies of Farhaan's work, he always listened attentively to Farhaan's discussions about his projects and clients. He knew how important it was for Farhaan to have someone to share his work pressures with, and he was more than willing to be that person. Apu told him about how Kerala had not changed since his last visit and how he was able to naturally connect with his homeland even after so many years. Then, Apu shared details about the progress of his stage play and how his students were becoming more enthusiastic, respecting him, and absorbing what he was trying to teach them. The hours passed and they realized how deeply they cherished these moments of connection, even from a distance.

As the conversation continued, Apu's voice sounded a bit melancholic, and Farhaan sensed his unease. He probed gently, asking if something was bothering him.

Apu hesitated for a moment before confiding, "It's just...being back here in my homeland... last night, I had memories flooding back from when I left this place. I was thinking about my last Kathakali performance here, and everything in my mind was so vivid."

"You miss your family, don't you?" Farhaan asked, understanding the depths of Apu's emotions.

Apu nodded, a hint of sadness in his eyes. "Yes, I do. But my father is no more, and my brother has taken over the family responsibilities. I do miss them."

Farhaan gently suggested, "Maybe you should go visit them once before you leave. It might help."

Apu hesitated, unsure about the idea. "I don't know. It's been so long, and things have changed."

Farhaan looked at Apu intently and said, "Don't let the weight of memories hold you back. Sometimes, revisiting the past can help heal the present."

A smile tugged at the corners of Apu's lips as he gazed at Farhaan through the screen. "You always know how to put things into perspective, don't you?"

Farhaan grinned, "Well, someone has to keep you in line." and he blurted out, "You know I love you, right?"

Apu smiled warmly, "Yes, and I love you too, and thank you for everything you have done for me."

Farhaan pretended to be offended and said with mock seriousness, "Oh, be careful with your gratitude. Remember, I can get there in five hours!"

Apu burst into laughter, and they both knew that distance could never diminish the love they had for each other.

X

The thoughts of how badly I treated Simran choked me with guilt that night. I often picked her up from a corner of the street and brought her to my room while drunk. This was just to prove how manly I was, and I would take advantage of her without considering how she felt. As soon as I satisfied my thirst, I threw her out. She was nothing more than an object for me to satisfy my carnal desires. A body that I could buy and use as I wish. But for the first time, I realized the woman in her, the innocent within her, and humanity within her. She was like a goddess I failed to pray all this time, even though I do not believe in gods. Seeing her in this light made me realize what kind of creature I had become.

I could see anxiety in her eyes as I quickly rose from the floor. I kneeled in front of her, and she stared at me with heightened anticipation.

"Do you remember you once told me about one of your clients who helped the poor or lower caste people in his town with their burials? You said it was tragic when he buried a lonely man who had committed suicide. There was no one to mourn him or bury him properly."

"Yaqoob, he visited me last week. Why him?"

Simran scowled at me, her eyes filled with curiosity. Yaqoob worked in a graveyard. However, his work extended beyond the daily rituals and cemetery maintenance. Yaqoob dedicated himself to helping the underprivileged people in his town who struggled to provide a proper burial for their loved ones.

In many communities, the cost of a funeral and burial can be overwhelming, leaving some families unable to give their departed members a dignified farewell. Yaqoob recognized this issue and assisted those with financial constraints or other difficulties. His compassion and empathy led him to establish a system that helped families in need. He worked tirelessly to ensure no one was left without a proper burial. He would guide grieving families through the legal procedures and paperwork required for a funeral, offering his expertise and support during their time of need.

"I have nothing more in this life. I have lived a life out of my control and shattered. Now I want to die in peace. Can you talk to him and arrange my death? I don't want to cause trouble for anyone around me. And if I die here, it'll create a huge mess."

I felt her kick reverberate in my chest as she rushed to the door. Slithering behind her, I grabbed her feet, wrapped my arms around her and pushed her against the door. She grimaced in pain from my grip and pungent stench. She tried to resist, pushing back against me, but I was too strong for her.

"I am no murderer."

She clenched her teeth together, her strength pushing me away as she whispered. Her voice was low but her message was clear. I could feel her anger in that single moment, the intensity of her emotions radiating outward like a shockwave. The desperation in her eyes was clear, her desperation to make me understand.

"Please... please, I want you to help me. I am a fucking coward, a shit of no use to anyone. And even if you don't help me, someday I will be found dead in this room as my regrets and shame will choke me to death."

I pleaded with her, tears streaming down my face. Slowly, I got down to my knees and wrapped both my arms tightly around her legs. My face was deep buried in her saree and I sobbed like a child, refusing to let her go without her acceptance.

"I came into this world without trouble and want to leave silently. Please... help me with this."

She pushed me back, her face etched with uncertainty and worry. I bowed my head and felt sorrow grip me. My pain deepened, like a bottomless well I had no hope of escaping. I wanted to speak, but my throat was too tight for words. All I could do was sit there, utterly helpless and alone as she watched me sink into my misery.

Simran took out her phone and walked towards the lift. As she approached, the landlord, an old man in his early 70s, walked in and frowned at me. He looked like he was about to burst out in anger. However, he must have caught a glimmer of pity in my eyes, as if he felt sorry for how pathetic I looked. I felt my stomach twist and turn, and could only lay there, frozen in place, as the landlord continued to stare.

"Are you OK?"

He asked his question in a low, polite voice. His eyes scanning the room for signs of life, taking in the sparse furnishings and the piles of books and papers that littered the room. He seemed to be searching for something, though what he was looking for was unclear. After a few moments, he seemed satisfied and his eyes settled on me.

"Drink some water."

It felt more like a warning. I sniffled, rubbed my nose and eyes to wipe away the tears, and swallowed a large gulp of water.

"Your rent for the past six months is still due. I want you to vacate this place in a week."

He walked inside and placed some legal documents on the desk.

"You sign these documents when you are alright and give them to security." And he walked away.

I felt a mix of emotions as I watched the old, frail body slowly lower into the elevator. Fear, exhaustion, and confusion all washed over me and I could feel my face contort to match the emotions. Simran was still on the phone, her face twisted into an angry stare. I stood at the entrance, meeting her eyes with a look of apology.

To calm my nerves, I lit a cigarette and inhaled deeply. The sky was almost orange now from my window and the birds were flying back to their nests. I felt a strange happiness welling up inside me, knowing I was about to leave this world, I wondered if all men experienced this same joy in their last moments.

She walked back, stood by my side near the window and lit her own cigarette. Smoke drifted up to the ceiling and I could sense her eyes still burning with anger. Her eyes lingered on me. I didn't know what to say, so I just stood there, awkward and quiet. We stayed like that for an eternity, neither of us willing to break the silence. Eventually, she turned away and the moment passed.

"I spoke to him, and he said he would share his address. And I have convinced him to take care of the rest."

I said nothing, but smiled politely. My eyes sparkled with amusement and fear, and my lips curved slightly upward.

"You have a phone right?" she asked.

I carefully removed my phone from the shelf, tucked inside a box. The phone was an old-fashioned one with rubber keypads, and I dropped it a few times, causing it to open up. To make sure it stayed shut, I carefully wound the tape around it, ensuring it was firmly secured.

"I just need to charge this device, and you can call anyone across the globe."

I smiled at her, but she looked awkwardly in my direction, her attention lingering on the phone in my hand.

"I want you to do another favor. I have set up a price for my old Mercedes, it's considered a gem now and still holds its appeal. I will send you the money through Yaqoob once it's sold. Please pay the rent due to the old man who just walked in and take the rest for yourself."

"I didn't know it was a Mercedes you picked me up in. It looked like crap."

"It is almost 15 years old now." We both giggled at the situation.

"I am not doing this for free either. I want something in return."

She demanded with a determined look on her face, her voice strong and unwavering. I could see a slight trace of tears on the edge of her eyes, shining in the pale light of the room. I shook my head, unable to deny her demands.

"I have a girl with me who doesn't deserve the life we live here. And I am giving her to you. Take care of her for one night and you can drop her tomorrow at the airport."

"But who is behind her? I don't want trouble."

"I don't want you to ask questions. In any case, you are dead, so why does it matter? Stay sober for a night and care for the bird."

I breathed out a long, steady stream of smoke through the window, my eyes tracking her silhouette in the darkness. She began to move with graceful ease and her hair swayed in the air. As I watched her disappear into the night, I felt a profound sense of admiration and appreciation. She had become a special part of my life, and I was thankful for this connection. My cigarette was held loosely in my fingers, smoke drifting around me, as I enjoyed the beauty of the moment.

"Why are you helping me after all the harm I have caused you? How do you trust me?"

She stopped at the door. After taking a moment to compose herself, she finally replied.

"Men are truly cursed with the unfortunate reality that, when their sexual needs are not satisfied, their dreams can become filled with unimaginable horrors. Men may find themselves dreaming of having sex with people in their own family, a situation entirely out of their control. It's true that throughout history, women have not been given the respect and rights they deserve. Women have been used for pleasure and entertainment, and even seen as disposable. Curse words used in various languages are often derived from words related to women. It's a mentality passed down through generations. Maybe men in the past were scared of women because they believed women were stronger than them. They created a stereotype of a life where women were dominated by men. Women are supposed to be soft and men are supposed to be tougher. We grow up listening to these stories and forget to realize who we really are."

"It is not your mistake, it is a common curse that all men face throughout their lives. But a man who has no control over his lust may end up losing tons of beautiful things in this world. But you, I know what you really are. Trying to prove yourself something you are not. You are not harmful, you are just broken. And so we all are."

The room was already dark with the evening sun setting, and I couldn't clearly see her face. But I could feel her emotion from that distance, like an invisible tether that connected us. I watched as she walked away into darkness like a fairy tale. I felt a pang of sadness as I watched her vanish.

Sometimes in life, we experience a peculiar sensation deep within us. It's like an instinctual awareness, a gut feeling that something significant is about to happen. This feeling becomes particularly poignant when we sense that it might be the last time we will ever see someone. I remember vividly that day when I felt this inexplicable energy surrounding me. It was as if the universe itself hinted at an impending goodbye. Deep down, I knew I would never see Simran again.

XI

As Maya woke up, her eyes partially opened to check her mobile phone, a bright glare greeted her vision. Despite the brightness, this had become her morning routine. After scanning her phone for any important messages, she casually tossed it behind her onto the bed. Her eyes then settled on a bunch of black-dyed cotton wastes sitting on a nearby chair. These cotton wastes were a common sight in her house, as her aunt worked in a cotton mill and brought them home for cleaning purposes. Maya had collected these cottons to sponsor a play she and her theater group were working on. The play aimed to break taboos around sex education, and these cottons were meant to represent pubic hair, creatively glued onto cardboard-shaped penises and vaginas. The sight of the cotton brought a smile to her face, reminding her of the exciting day ahead at the theater.

Maya lived with her aunt after her father and elder brother died in an accident when she was only 14 years old. That tragic incident marked the last time her aunt saw Maya cry. The young girl had no memories of her mother either, as she had left her at a very tender age. Throughout her childhood, various speculations circulated among family and neighbors about her mother's whereabouts.

Some suggested she had an affair with another man, while others claimed she had met with a brutal accident. There were whispers about her mental health, with some believing she was secretly sent to an asylum. Shockingly, a few even speculated that she had joined bandits fighting against the government.

Yet, each time such gossip reached Maya's ears, she couldn't help but visualize her late father's face. His expression seemed to blend sadness with a tinge of embarrassment, a mix of emotions that puzzled her greatly. Unable to decipher her father's feelings, she hesitated to probe further into the mystery of her mother's disappearance. Deep down, she was certain that her father harbored some level of disappointment whenever discussions about her mother arose. As the years passed, Maya gradually lost her curiosity about her mother, accepting that some questions were best left unanswered.

With great hesitation and a few stretches, Maya finally roused herself from bed. She stood in the living space, waiting for her aunt to leave the kitchen so she could make her own coffee. The strained silence between them had persisted for three long years, originating from an incident in Maya's high school days.

It all began when the school principal called Maya's guardian, her aunt, to discuss her behavior at school. Maya had always found it easier to connect with boys rather than girls. She thrived in their company, engaging in sports, and occasionally beating them when the situation called for it. Growing up in a household dominated by male presence, she felt more at ease spending time with men. The idea of wearing dresses never appealed to her, and she would often borrow her late brother's clothes, finding comfort in their loose fit and casual style.

Despite not being highly sociable, her chance encounter with a transgender woman at a bus stop forged a connection. As they exchanged friendly waves, Maya felt an instant bond with this stranger. They soon became fast friends, exchanging chocolates and engaging in long conversations every evening. Maya would often forgo taking the bus, instead walking home accompanied by her newfound friend.

As her friendship with the transgender woman blossomed, Maya faced inquiries from her teacher about her after-school activities and her preference for male company. Unable to articulate her feelings, Maya found herself at a loss for words. When her aunt discovered the nature of Maya's friendships, she unleashed a torrent of frustration and criticism. She launched into a heated rant, listing the sacrifices she had made for Maya's education and the love she had poured into raising her after the tragic loss of her family. She couldn't understand why Maya insisted on defying societal norms, behaving like a boy, and befriending someone they considered 'different'. The gossip mongers in the neighborhood further fueled the fire, insinuating that Maya's supposed deviant behavior had been inherited from her missing mother. Some individuals took the gossip to an even more malicious level, spreading rumors that Maya was seen hanging around with a boy after school. They painted her actions as sinful, casting judgment on her innocent friendships and innocent encounters. The whispers grew louder, creating a cloud of negativity around her, tarnishing her reputation in the eyes of those who were quick to condemn without understanding.

After the incident, her bus stand friend she had bonded with, seemed to have vanished from her life. Despite their daily interactions and the strong connection they had formed, Maya never saw her again. However, instead of harboring resentment, she felt a sense of pity for those who misunderstood her. Understanding that their ignorance stemmed from innocence, she chose to distance herself from the negativity, creating a cocoon of tranquility and positivity around her. Within the walls of her self-created world, Maya withdrew from the outside noise, including her own family members. Despite living in the same house, the once lively conversations with her aunt had dwindled, replaced by an unspoken tension. Maya's silence was her armor, protecting her from the disapproving glances and unsolicited opinions.

Completing her school education, Maya decided against attending college, convinced that the atmosphere there would not align with her belief in positive energy. Maya's belief in positive energy became her guiding principle as she navigated through life. She sought out environments and people that exuded a sense of goodness and kindness, yearning for the same positive energy she once felt when her father and brother were alive. She sought solace in books, immersing herself in the wisdom and stories they offered. The world of literature became her sanctuary, providing her with the good energy she craved. Embracing her passion for spreading and seeking for positive energy, Maya found purpose in joining an NGO that focused on promoting awareness and understanding of LGBTQ+ issues. Her involvement in organizing thought-provoking events further enriched her understanding of the world and strengthened her commitment to creating a more accepting society. As fate would have it, Maya's dedication and warmth caught the attention of a friend, Bejoy, who recommended her to give tours to foreign visitors in their city. This opportunity not only exposed her to new cultures and perspectives but also served as a conduit for the positive energy she was looking for.

As her aunt finally stepped out of the kitchen with her lunch box, she scowled at Maya, a sight that had become all too familiar. Without missing a beat, Maya walked into the kitchen to make her coffee, smoothly avoiding any confrontation. While she found her aunt's disapproval rather cute and innocent, she couldn't deny that her aunt's negative energy affected her mental well-being. Maya recognized the importance of protecting her inner peace and chose not to engage in arguments with negative energies, opting instead to stay silent.

Their home often played host to curious visitors who bombarded Maya with questions about her appearance and choices. But she had become adept at handling such inquiries, noticing a common thread among them all. Some would inquire about her short hair, others about her boyish mannerisms, and there were those who questioned her decision not to attend college or her involvement with an NGO. Amidst these prying questions, some even dared to question her gender identity. In response, Maya adopted a humble smile and a gracious demeanor. She had her own tactics to maintain her peace, often choosing to listen to rock music while discreetly covering her ears with her hair. Gently nodding along to their lip movements, she avoided any unnecessary conversations.

Seated on the entrance stair, Maya relished the pleasant climate that lingered in the air after last night's rain. Her fingers glided over her mobile screen, scrolling through messages and notifications. In a matter of seconds, her excitement became palpable as she stumbled upon an email that changed the course of her moment.

Amidst her part-time commitments at the NGO and theater, Maya had been diligently applying for positions in other NGOs outside Kerala. Her heart yearned for a chance to work with a larger community of like-minded individuals, united by a common purpose. But it was a particular email from a national-level company in Himachal Pradesh that set her soul on fire. The email informed her that she had been accepted to join their team of volunteers, dedicated to rescuing and supporting all those affected by society's injustices. The prospect of being part of such a meaningful endeavor was a dream come true for Maya. More than just the allure of the job, it was the opportunity to live amidst the serene mountains that filled her heart with elation. Maya had always dreamed of escaping from the confines of her current location, wanting to relieve her aunt of the burden she felt she had become.

Without a moment's hesitation, she typed a swift reply to the email, expressing her profound gratitude for the opportunity and stating her availability to join anytime during the next week.

From the garden, her aunt's eyes fixated on Maya, her mind filled with curiosity about the source of her niece's excitement. Despite witnessing Maya in this euphoric state on multiple occasions, the aunt wondered what had sparked such enthusiasm this time. As her niece spoke to herself, a habitual quirk that often made her blush with amusement, the aunt found herself torn between wanting to share in Maya's joy and the fear of the judgment that others had implanted in her mind.

Maya's excitement and anticipation swirled within her, urging her to share the incredible news with someone close to her heart. Her fellow artists from the theater were the first people who came to mind. Among them, Apu, with his warm presence and positive energy, had recently left a strong impression on her, even if it was only a brief encounter. As she opened the WhatsApp group to share her news, she hesitated, realizing that this moment deserved more than just a digital message. Determined to celebrate with her team in person, she quickly erased the three lines she had typed and made her way to her room. She carefully gathered the dyed cottons she had sponsored for the theater. Amidst the cottons, she carefully tucked in a six-foot-long pride-colored flag that she had been planning to stitch into a cape, a symbol of her unwavering support to wear during the rally.

***

Although Maya loved her work and always found herself excited about what she did, she had never been punctual for work. She found it hard to wake up in the morning after staying up late at night, either engrossed in the books she read or binge-watching TV shows. She was also terrible at remembering routes and bus numbers, often ending up on the wrong bus halfway through her journey, only realizing her mistake when she had to convince the bus driver to stop so she could detour and catch the right bus. At times, she would doze off into a power nap during her morning rides, losing herself in profound music, only to awaken at an unknown stop.

When she reached the theater, Apu, along with other artists, had nearly finished cleaning the stage, sweeping the floors, and removing dust from every possible place. Apu greeted Maya with a nod and a gentle smile, never complaining about her punctuality. The fellow artists began their stretching and warm-up exercises, as physical activity was part of their routine, while Apu continued to dust off the benches and fans.

He hung the cloth he used for cleaning over his shoulders and caught the crew's attention with a clap. They gathered on the stage while Apu remained on the floor.

"We've been practicing a lot, and our play is just a few days away—the big day, I believe." Apu had a habit of smiling at the person he was addressing after finishing a sentence.

"Today, let's try something different." He clasped his hands and carefully assessed the energy of each crew member.

The crew stood perplexed, wondering what Apu had in store for them. However, a pulse of excitement shone in their eyes, knowing that Apu was about to teach them something new and valuable, fueled by the respect they had for him.

"We either love our work or are forced into it. Amidst it all, we tend to forget the beauty of life, the fascination of the world around us. I'm not talking about the glamorous images of Europe you see on the internet. I mean the world right here around you—the flowers, the diverse people, the various voices. The way the air touches your face at different times of the day. The ever-changing colors of the sky that shift like a chameleon and the melodies of birds with every passing minute. We often overlook the tiny beauties that nature offers us while we keep running through our lives because we feel we have to."

The crew exchanged murmurs among themselves, their curiosity beaming. Apu then called over the lady who cleaned the theater, asking her to leave a bucket of soapy water and a mop in the corner and take a day off.

He continued, "As an actor, it's essential to understand how to portray a character convincingly. However, simply embodying a character isn't enough to be a true actor. You must cultivate knowledge and wisdom. You must teach yourself kindness and compassion. You have to observe yourself and the world around you with love and respect. You must become anything the script demands, whether it's a gust of wind or even a solid rock. As an actor, you need to comprehend the subtleties of human emotions and empathize with your fellow actors. An actor should embody discipline and be a good human being."

Apu walked towards the entrance door, opening it to let the sunlight stream in and touch the floor.

"Today, I want all of you to step outside this room. Don't rush; there's no need to hurry. Observe everything around you. As actors, you must be aware of the interconnectedness of human emotions. Have you ever studied the psychology of movies and theater? It's not easy to captivate thousands of people for three straight hours. What keeps a moviegoer engaged? Our curiosity. Each person watches and interprets a movie based on their life experiences, with their unique perceptions. As an actor, you must learn to grasp this curiosity; otherwise, your art remains lifeless, like a dead bird."

"How do we learn this? Where should we go?" One of the crew members inquired.

"Take a bus or any form of transportation. Observe the diverse people you encounter. Try to imagine their lives, the challenges they might face. If you see a man carrying a bag, ponder the person who might have crafted it. What could their story be? Are they making a bag right now? Alternatively, sit in a park and watch the sky above or people passing by. Try to envision their stories and explore intriguing characters. Any other questions?"

"So, no practice today, is that confirmed?" Maya asked.

Apu shook his head with a tender smile and said, "Disperse for now. See you all tomorrow." Then he walked toward the bucket with soapy water, eager to clean the entire theater on his own.

XII

I waited at the same place where I picked up Simran in the late hours of the night. I expected to see Simran again, but she was nowhere to be found. At first, I was uncertain about the girl—it seemed like Simran had passed on all my character knowledge to her. I was completely taken aback when a young woman suddenly appeared and hopped into my car. She tossed her duffle bag into the back seat without saying a word. I just stared at her, with a huge question mark in my mind. She looked around nervously, as if she was in a hurry. I again glanced at her out of the corner of my eye, and I could see that she was clearly uncomfortable in that place. I decided to act and started my car's engine, and we drove away.

She had a faint air of desperation in her eyes, and a hint of anxiety in her breath. The girl was oddly dressed for a summer night in Chennai. Her gray hoodie zipped up to her neck, the California logo embroidered on it. Beneath the hoodie, she wore a saree, like Simran wore. Simran had called her 'the bird', but looking at her now, she seemed much more mature than I had expected. She had thick skin and appeared to be in her mid-20s. Her face was pale with fear, and there was no makeup. I noticed her eyes were constantly wandering with nervousness, and her smell was nothing special, so my car was not filled with any distinctive aroma. She was an ethereal figure with an aura of mystery surrounding her.

The atmosphere inside the car was heavy and silent for the first 10 minutes; the only sound was the whooshing of the engine, the indicator signal as I changed direction, and the occasional honking of passers-by. Her eyes darted around the streets, never settling on one point. She held her fists tightly together and shook her legs nervously, an outward sign of her inner turmoil. I watched her for a few moments, and then broke the silence.

"Where do you want to go?"

She didn't respond, just sat there expressionless. This was as if she hadn't heard me or I didn't exist at all.

"Do you want to go to my place?"

My body tingled when she scowled at me with anger and fear. It was clear that my question was totally inappropriate for the occasion. Who could blame her for being angry when a man who looked as disheveled and untrustworthy as I did called her to his place? It must have seemed like I was a rapist or a serial killer.

"Did you eat?" I posed my next question, hoping she could answer it.

Her lips formed a thin line as she shook her head slowly from side to side.

"Do you want dinner?"

She said nothing again and remained still, frozen in place. I was famished and decided it would be wise to forgo any more questioning and simply focus on filling my rumbling stomach.

I parked my car at a familiar spot on a food street, where I intended to have my dinner. I was surprised to find the food street empty during the week. On weekends, the place is usually bustling with people of all ages, the atmosphere is filled with laughter and joy, and finding a parking spot can be quite a challenge. We stepped into the small Chinese stall, cigarette in my hand, and she followed me behind. I wasn't sure what she would like to eat, so I decided to take the initiative and order for us. I asked the girl behind the counter for two servings of soupy ramen and a plate of chilli beef as a side. As I paid for the food, I could feel her eyes on me, watching my every move. Nervousness was written all over her face as she bit her nails anxiously. Her body shook uncontrollably and I could sense her discomfort. I decided to occupy myself with my cigarette, not wanting to add to her distress by staring at her or asking questions.

She ate the noodles hungrily, savoring every bite, seemingly oblivious to the world around her. The food aroma wafted through the air. Her lips curved at the edges in a small smile as she closed her eyes in delight. I pulled out another cigarette from the carton, the smoke swirling around me as I watched her seemingly lost in a parallel world and observed her innocence. She didn't seem to intend to leave me a single piece of beef, as she kept taking more noodles.

We finished our dinner and returned to my car. I took a deep breath and started the engine, trying to clear my head of all the anxiety building up inside me. I had never been in this kind of situation before and it was overwhelming. I glanced in the rearview mirror and saw the 3 empty cigarette packets I had thrown out of my pocket, now lying on the ground. I drove away, not knowing where I was headed, but I knew I had to leave that place.

It felt like an eternity since we started, but it was barely an hour. As we drove through Chennai's western part, the streets were filled with small hotels that ran all night. The night was welcomed with joyous energy by people of all ages, seemingly relieved to unburden themselves of the pressures of the day. Young boys were gathered in groups, playing multiplayer video games on their mobile phones. The tea shops were filled with couples drinking juices, while teenagers smoked and argued with each other. On the stairs of a temple, we saw some elderly men sitting shirtless and cursing the summer air. All around, people were engaging in different activities, each enjoying the night in their own way. The traffic police were also out in full force, bribing people for various reasons. Everything was chaotic. The night was still and the car was filled with peaceful silence. Outside, city lights shone brightly, casting reflections on our faces.

Her wide eyes reflected the city view as she sat quietly lazing in the window. There was no trace of a smile on her face. Instead, there was a hollow emptiness in her gaze that seemed to suggest she was struggling to find something that she could not.

I stopped at a signal, and two boys on a motorcycle stopped beside the car. They were mesmerized by the girl's look. She seemed to be in a trance-like state until the boys arrived, and suddenly snapped out of it. The girl quickly pulled her hoodie up and tried to avoid eye contact with them. I could sense her fear, and stretched out to her side to let her know she was safe. I pressed my lips together and motioned her to close the manual louver of the window glass. She complied with a slight wheeze, and I stared at the boys until they drove away.

After driving for another hour, I decided to stop near an old movie theater. I asked her if we could spend some time watching a movie, and she agreed. I wanted her to feel safe, so I reassured her that we were far away from her place and that there was no chance of anyone recognizing her.

The theater was dimly lit, with a huge crack running along the screen edge. An unpleasant smell filled the air, and our feet crunched over spilled popcorn and empty Coke cans. It was clear that the theater had not been properly cleaned after the previous show. We could barely see the damaged seats and sticky floors, and the entire place had an air of disarray. It was obvious that no one had been here for a while, and the mess left behind had been forgotten. We arrived 10 minutes late. Our seats were in the middle row in the top left corner. We noticed that there were very few people in the theater, sitting in random seats.

I couldn't understand why the audience was so excited by the immature content playing in front of me. It was a chaotic scene; cars were burned unnecessarily, men flew in the air after being punched, and the crowd cheered for it. I felt pathetic as I sank into my chair and watched in amazement. I wondered why people found this to be such an entertaining thing to watch. It seemed like there was something more to it than what I saw. It made no sense to me.

My eyes directed at the girl. I stared at her for a few moments, taking in her features illuminated by the colors of the film. She seemed so taken by what was happening on the screen, and I couldn't help but smile at the sheer joy and excitement radiating from her. It appeared as though this was her first theater experience. I wanted to let her enjoy the film in peace, so I sank deeper into my seat. Feeling my eyelids grow heavy and before I knew it, I drifted off into peaceful sleep.

***

I felt a sudden thud in my seat. Jolting out of my sleep, I realized I had taken the deepest power nap I had had in a long time. I was glad for the boring movie playing on the screen in front of me, which allowed me to drift off into a deep sleep. Slowly stretching my legs, I noticed the girl had disappeared. As I searched across the theater, I watched her quickly run out of the exit door illuminated with a dim red light. She was in a hurry and didn't look back. I heard an intense sound behind me. When I looked around, I saw a boy and a girl engulfed in a passionate embrace. His leg became entangled with hers as he stretched from his chair to hers, and his hand slipped inside her pants. Neither of them seemed to know my presence as they continued to kiss deeply.

I searched for the girl, running around the corner of the theater, past store fronts and alleyways. Looked for the bird in every nook and cranny, but she was nowhere in sight. My feet hurt from all the running, so I stopped to take a break and catch my breath in the parking lot and ran again. The darkness seemed oppressive, and I was almost startled by the sudden sound of a dog howling under an orange streetlight in the distance. I glanced at my watch and saw that it was twelve past fifteen in the night. My anxiety lifted me up as I had no idea where she had disappeared.

I kept walking, looking around for a glimpse of her, but all I could see was an empty street ahead of me. Luckily, I found her as I walked past the metro entrance. She was sitting there quietly, with an air of loneliness surrounding her. As I touched her shoulder, she jolted and turned towards me with shock and fear. The tears that had flowed down her cheeks frozen and her eyes widened as she saw me there. I stood there awkwardly, not knowing what to do. My mind wanted me to comfort her and let her know I was there for her, but I was too scared to move. The silence was deafening and I felt suffocated. I wanted to say something kind, but the words got stuck in my throat. I tried to take a deep breath but something blocked me from breathing. I finally said, "It's okay, I'm here for you."

I was taken aback by her sudden outburst. Her hands were clenched in a tight fist and her screams echoed throughout the empty city. No matter how hard I tried to comfort her, her screams only got louder and more desperate. I was powerless to do anything but stand there and watch her. Her screaming never subsided, her body still trembled with emotion. I stepped forward to talk to her, but she quickly stepped back and shouted, "GO AWAY! GO AWAY!" I could sense fear in her voice.

I never expected to be in such an awkward situation. I was standing by her, who was clearly distressed, and suddenly a few men driving by stopped and tried to push me away. It was almost as if I was doing something wrong by being there. Not only did I console the girl, but also reason with these so-called "superheroes". A crowd formed around us, and people from opposite lanes stared in confusion.

I ran as fast as I could towards the tea stall nearby, desperate to buy a water bottle. My feet pounded against the pavement and I could feel sweat dripping under my shirt. When I finally got there, I grabbed a bottle and hurried back towards the girl. The closer I got, the more terror I exhaled. Her hair was completely disheveled and wild, saliva dripped down her mouth, and her eyes were smudged with mascara. My heart raced and my body trembled as I stood there, gazing at her in fear.

I tried to keep my distance while offering her the water bottle. Unfortunately, she was in no mood to accept my help and threw anything she could find at me and the people around me. Everyone was shocked and taken aback. I wanted to give her time to process and accept what had happened. So, I convinced the crowd to disperse, understanding that their presence would only distress her further. I placed the water bottle near her and decided to look after her from a distance and walked away.

I kept smoking, one cigarette after another without a break. As I did, my eyes settled into a routine, never straying from the clear dark sky, the vibrant red lights of a passing motorcycle, and the state of her. It was as if I was trying to take in and imprint every single detail, my eyes staying fixed on the same point until I finished my seventh cigarette chain. Even then, anxiety lingered, and I felt like I could have stayed there, smoking one cigarette after the other, forever.

When I dropped my seventh cigarette, I saw her there, wiping tears from her face. She picked up the water bottle I had placed next to her. I slowly ambled in her direction, asking if I should stop a taxi for her. She seemed uncomfortable with my presence and I wasn't sure why. However, she nodded in approval, still wiping the water from her mouth.

I had no courage to ask her to come with me, so I decided not to force her. As she sat there on the stairs of the metro entrance, seemingly lost in her own thoughts and emotions, I stood at the edge of the pavement, waiting for some form of transportation to take her away safely. Suddenly I heard her voice for the first time that night.

"Do you know any place near, where there is no trace of humans, or their ugly voices? In a place where a heavy rock sits in sadness admiring the earth's rotation, a rock that never sleeps and talking to crows that visit her? Can you drive me to this place?"

Her voice was gruff, yet gentle. Her question and the somberness in her tone left me speechless, and I froze in place, feeling dejected and unable to respond. I stayed there, my disappointment tangible in the air. The silence lingered between us, a reminder of my inability to find words to express my feelings. The moment seemed to stretch endlessly, until I could muster a response.

I said yes. To be honest, I had no idea such a place existed.

XIII

Later that evening, after a long and intense day of practice, Apu found himself at a crossroads. For years, he had wrestled with the idea of facing his past, of revisiting the place he had left. Now, standing at the threshold of his childhood home, he felt a mixture of excitement and trepidation. The decision to return had not been an easy one. He had spent hours playing out various scenarios in his mind, weighing the potential consequences of each choice.

The building, as he approached, stood as a testament to time. Its terracotta hut with its ancient charm welcomed him back with open arms. The sprawling garden, once his mother's pride and joy, still thrived, enveloping the house in a lush sea of greenery. Apu's heart swelled with nostalgia as he recognized most of the plants he had grown up with, each carrying memories of his childhood. But a pang of sorrow struck him as he noticed the absence of the majestic mango tree that had once graced the landscape. He wondered why it had been cut down and felt an ache in his heart for the loss of a cherished symbol from his past.

As he stood there, the weight of time bore down on him. Twenty-three years had passed, yet the memories felt as vivid as ever. The echoes of laughter and the warmth of his mother's embrace enveloped him, drawing him into a whirlwind of emotions. He took a deep breath, inhaling the familiar scents of the earth and the blossoms, and he felt a sense of belonging that he had long suppressed. Stepping closer, memories flooded his mind like a torrential downpour. He could almost hear the sound of his father's voice, the gentle rustling of the leaves, and the laughter of his friends echoing through the walls. It was as if time had stood still in this small pocket of his past.

A small breeze swept through, carrying the distant laughter of children playing outside. As he stood there, lost in memories, a small boy rushed from the hallway and stood in front of him, seeking his attention. The boy scowled, questioning Apu about his presence in their home. Apu explained that he had come to visit a man named Unni, and the boy asked him to wait inside the house while he went to fetch his father.

Summoning all his courage, he pushed the door open, and the scent of incense and home-cooked meals enveloped him. The familiar sight of the living room greeted him and the walls adorned with photographs of his family. His gaze settled on the picture of his parents, their loving smiles and stares frozen in time. Emotion welled up inside him, and he paid his respects to the ones who had shaped him into the person he had become. The open hall in the center of the house beckoned him, just as it had done when he was a young boy. Apu took a seat on the floor, feeling the coolness of the terracotta tiles against his skin. He looked up at the sky through the grilled roof, its colors slowly transitioning from warm hues to a canvas of deep blue speckled with stars.

Darkness embraced the world outside, but the silence of the house seemed to grow, offering him a moment of solitude. Apu's thoughts drifted back to another past, his mind landed on a pivotal moment when he had confessed to his father his desire to withdraw as a Kathakali artist, to go to Mumbai, and become an actor. His father had firmly opposed the idea, believing that Apu's destiny was intricately tied to the family legacy as the greatest "katha" (artist) of their village. Unable to bear the weight of expectation, Apu had left home the next morning, embarking on a path he believed was meant for him. With a heavy heart, he recalled the conversation he had just had with his brother, Unni. The hurtful words, the judgment, and the disdain had pierced him deeply, reminding him of the rift that had grown between them over the years.

As Apu waited, his heart beat faster with anticipation, unsure of what awaited him. When Unni finally walked in, their eyes locked, and the years between them seemed to fade away, if only for a moment. Unni's eyes held a mix of surprise, disbelief, and perhaps a hint of nostalgia. He studied Apu's appearance—the graying hair, the beard, the sunken body and contrasted it with his own. Unni had inherited their father's features, with black-dyed hair and a protruding jaw. Apu smiled as Unni's son who was introduced as Shaji and was named by their father, finding the boy's resemblance to his younger self endearing.

"What brings you here?" Unni's question was direct, but betraying his emotions. He then disregarded looking at Apu, and he proceeded directly to the tap in the center of their house to wash his hands and feet.

Apu found it difficult to maintain eye contact with his brother. His throat tightened, and he struggled to find the right words. "I came here for a theater play and thought I would visit you."

"Well, it seems you are no longer an actor. The entire village was abuzz with gossip about your controversies that were broadcasted on all TV channels. I'm glad father wasn't alive to see that."

Unni's face hardened. The accusations stung, and Apu was unable to bear the burden of his brother's disappointment. Unni's words struck Apu like arrows, each one piercing his heart with venom. Apu remained silent, unable to respond to the harsh accusations.

Amidst the tension, Unni's son stood by, observing the exchange between the two brothers. Apu found solace in the child's presence, a reminder of innocence and unconditional love. But Unni asked his son to leave, giving them privacy.

A smile crossed Apu's face despite being in a strange situation with his brother, and he said, "I too have a daughter. You want to see her; she is so lovely."

"I didn't know you were married. Is she an actress like you? Or... is she someone.. someone from whom you... raped?"

"No... no. It's not any of them... I didn't do any of... those harm to any girls." Apu's anxiety welled up, and a tear threatened to escape from the edge of his eyes.

Apu grabbed his mobile and showed his brother a selfie of himself, Farhaan, and Ruhi. With a thin layer of tears in his eyes, he pulled out a happy smile as he looked at the picture.

His brother glanced at the photo and asked, "Where is your wife?"

Apu walked back to his place and hesitated to reply. But moments later, Unni widened his eyes and understood the picture. Unni's expression turned incredulous, and his words dripped with disapproval, "How can... how can you marry... a man? How can you have a... daughter with a man?"

"We adopted Ruhi together, and we love her unconditionally," Apu calmly explained, bracing himself for Unni's reaction.

"God save us! Father treated us both the same way. He gave us enough respect, he taught us the same things. How can you be this... ruined?"

Apu struggled to convey that his feelings for Farhaan were no different from Unni's feelings for his wife. However, he chose to remain silent, realizing that some things couldn't be explained.

"Father had a good reputation here. Our family is highly respected. Our theater is still running, and there are still people here who respect our culture, our tradition, our art. So please do not come here again and spoil everything that has been inherited."

A deep sadness washed over Apu as he realized that some bridges couldn't be mended. The chasm between his past and present seemed insurmountable. Grief and acceptance mingled within him as he acknowledged that he couldn't change the past, but he could learn from it. Apu nodded his head, trying to hold back his tears. He slowly walked outside the house, and as he was about to put on his shoes, his eyes met the lush green garden and what so ever laid in front of him for a moment. Yet, a glimmer of hope flickered in his heart. He turned swiftly and walked back inside the house, though his pace was now more deliberate as he approached his brother.

Unni stared at him with a confused look on his face. "Did you forget something?"

"I... I know I have disrespected our art... disrespected our culture, our tradition. But, I have done over... 12 films, and 8 of those are a huge success. I have also been doing several stage plays for the past 3 years. But none of those provided me the satisfaction that I felt here. The process we follow before the play... the connection with the crowd... the stories we tell them, it truly resonates with my soul... and that doesn't match any characters I have portrayed as an actor... or the money and properties I have accumulated."

"You cannot change what has happened," Unni's face remained impassive.

"I know, and I wish I could. But all I ask from you is to understand that I am not the same man anymore. So, all I ask is for the chance to do one last play here under our theater's name. I want to experience our crowd. I want to feel that sheer emotion once again... Would you please let me do that one last time?"

Unni looked fixedly at him for a few moments, his expression unreadable, but anger seeping through. Then, controlling his rage, he turned away and retreated inside the house, leaving Apu standing there, his heart heavy with unresolved feelings.

Apu stepped outside and he felt his emotions threaten to engulf him. The tears he had been holding back finally spilled, coursing down his cheeks. Starting the car engine, he kept driving, his head wobbling with anxiety all this time. He let out a long wheeze as he no longer tried to control his tears and let them fall freely. As he drove, he kept muttering to himself, and his voice slowly grew louder, "I will have my own play... I will have my own play... I will have my own play..."

XIV

We drove to a hill station a four-hour drive from Chennai where I remember visiting seven years ago. It wasn't anything particularly special, but I enjoyed the drive, winding through hairpin bends and taking in the crisp, clean air rare to find in the city. The views were breathtaking, and the peace and tranquility was a welcome respite from everyday life.

We never stopped on our journey. All she asked for was to lower her seat so she could lie down, but she never slept. The road was dark and my car's headlights were only partially working. I was worried I might hit someone while driving on hilly roads and along long stretches. The silence was strange and surreal. Ilayaraaja's songs played throughout the journey, making the atmosphere even more peculiar. In the middle of our trip, I decided to play some of my Rolling Stones songs to break the mood. We opened the car windows to let in the breeze, and I kept my right hand on the car's ceiling, a cigarette between my fingers.

There I was, driving in the pitch black night, the girl by my side, her expression neither fixed nor her gaze changing. Darkness pressed in around me. It was a feeling unlike anything I had experienced before. The night was still, nothing but the hum of the car engine and the occasional sound of a nocturnal animal to be heard. It was as if I was the only one on the planet, just me and my car. The dark night was my own personal realm.

We had climbed for hours, driving through 10 hairpin bends, the car winding up the cliff face, before she finally broke the silence. She asked me to park the car at the curve of one hairpin and I found a safe spot. We stepped out of the car and the place was pitch dark. The stars shone above us, sparkling in the night sky and providing us with some light to make out the shapes of the rocks around us.

Despite the roughness of the path, she started walking towards the place as if it were not foreign to her. I ran behind her, pulled my lighter trigger. As the cliff led to a dead end with only a few steps from the curb, we had little visibility ahead of ourselves. We took a few steps forward and could feel the chill in the air. I could see some faint lights flickering in the distance, coming from the matchbox-like houses I had seen earlier in the day. We continued trudging forward, hoping to find a way out of the darkness. The rock we had climbed over seemed like a wall that divided us from the unknown.The wind kept picking up and pushing us away. The darkness seemed to be getting thicker and thicker and it felt like we were getting further and further away from the light. We could barely see anything beyond the rock.

I had no idea what to do or say. I could feel my heart racing as I thought about what would happen if she jumped. I slowly moved the lighter towards her face, and I could see the sadness in her eyes, illuminated by the orange glow of the flames. She closed her eyes and wheezed, her cry growing louder with every breath. She reached out to me, gripping my shirt tightly. Her body shook with each sob and she bent over, her face covered in tears. I watched helplessly as her cries turned into a scream that echoed off into the darkness. It was a sound of agony, pain and rage. Her hands clenched into fists, her face contorted in sorrow and fear. All that surrounded her was darkness, emptiness and void. She cried for the pain she endured, screaming for all the hurt inflicted upon her.

For ten to fifteen minutes, I remained in that spot, observing her fight against sadness. But eventually, I knew I had to leave; it was too painful to stay. I started to walk away, but I was still scared she might jump, so I kept looking back until I reached my car. Even though I had moved twenty feet away, I could still hear her screams.

I lit my cigarette, smoke curling up into the night sky, and jumped over my car bonnet. I sat there, knowing this would take time, and kept my eyes alternating between her and the emptiness around me. The darkness swallowed up the huge space we were in, only heard by the occasional breeze rustle. As I gazed up into the night sky, I was captivated by the multitude of twinkling stars that sparkled like polka dots in the darkness. The sight was mesmerizing, and it reminded me of Simran. All of a sudden, I was struck by a strange feeling—death. I wondered what it would be like to be buried in the ground, to feel the soil pushed against my face. And it was strange that every time I engulfed my thoughts about death, a mixed feeling of happiness and sadness gushed over me.

My thoughts slowly drifted away, and I felt hollow. But then, I imagined the vibrant colors of the night sky, reminiscent of the galaxies I had seen in books. It felt like the sheer scale of the night sky opened up to me, allowing me to enter its mysterious world. It seemed like a painting, carefully crafted and filled with beauty.

***

I sensed a thud as she came back and sat on the edge of the car. Her presence next to me was surprising, but I didn't want to distract myself from my thoughts. Several minutes passed in silence, just being together as I lay on my car's windshield.

"What do you see above there?" Her voice sounded rough and melodious.

"It's like I'm a bird staring at the dome of our cage and the glistening stars are the rims. Or, I am trying to feel the enormous curve of this universe. I see myself swimming and floating through the clouds and pushing myself to reach up above to see this giant ball from the other side. What if I had this power?"

We remained silent for the next few minutes, trying to absorb what I said or feel this power. Afterward, she sang again.

"When you are walking on a busy road, have you ever imagined how that place would have looked 100 years ago, or during the caveman's time in the past? What would have been where these tiny shops were located? Or from where would they buy their clothes? Would they have time to be so fussy about them? Or if they were ruled by a king, how would that experience be? What kind of emotions would human beings have experienced in those days? Or I wonder how history would be sung if those giant trees who lived for centuries could write or sing a song about everything she has witnessed in her lifetime through a breeze?"

I replied to her thoughts, "I smoked weed once and it's a fascinating leaf. Our brain is always occupied or wandering by thoughts and multiple events. We think about what happened a week ago or what we need to do next month but our body is stuck in the present. And when you smoke this weed, your visualization power increases and all these events in your head appear real. It becomes tangled with thoughts that sometimes you forget the difference between reality and your imagination."

Taking off my glasses, I placed them on my car's roof behind me. My gaze latched up on the sky and I could feel she was chained there with me.

"Based on this thought, I once had a theory in my mind. What if there is a drug that takes you into a wild sleep where you feel nothing of this current world, like you are temporarily dead? Walking into a dream, everything is no longer scattered, but you can control anything around you. The drug takes you into another universe just like ours, where you walk like a newly born man and not a child. You get to live as the person you wish to be and create anything in the world as per your desires. But I also wondered what life would be like without pain. What would I write if sadness was absent?"

"Aren't we all trying some distractions to escape from this reality once in a while?" She replied and ambled towards the curb staring at the sky.

Then she said, "I was waiting for a train once and imagined feeling deaf? I suddenly felt a huge void in the place where I imagined I no longer heard the chaotic noises around me. Instead, I felt a pleasant void as if I had traveled through a pipe and transformed into an ant. What would an ant hear? And what if we human beings had a switch to control everything, for eyes to not see the unfortunate events, for ears to not listen to chaotic noises, for nose to not smell the unpleasant odor and a main switch for the heart to switch off our emotions? What if we had all the powers to design our own human race? And what if this train took me to the paradise I dreamt of?"

She lost herself in her thoughts, reflecting on the events of the day. It felt like her mind was spinning, her thoughts jumbling together.

"Where did this train take you?" I slowly looked at her, taking in every detail.

"To a beautiful city, Mumbai."

"And how old were you then?"

"I was just 17 years old, full of dreams, and terrified of starting over in an unfamiliar city."

I felt captivated by her story. It stirred a strange curiosity within me.

"I was eight years old when I served plastic plates at my mother's second wedding. Since then, all my life I have seen my mother getting beaten up by men and all her husbands treating me like a curse, except my father. I remember she once said he was nothing like her other two husbands. He was an innocent soul and maybe that is why God took him away from us. Growing up with my first stepfather, I experienced molestation when I was too young to understand. I remember nights when the only sound I could hear was my mother's moans coming from the bedroom. My mother's third husband was a domineering figure, and he seemed to resent me as if I was a reminder of my mother's past. As I grew up, I often imagined a paradise where the entire world was filled with women's laughter."

Her life's energy radiated around me as I curled up, my legs drawn close to my chest. Her eyes were fixed on some unknown point in the distance, but somehow it glowed without any hint of sadness.

"I arrived in a charming city with big dreams. My plan was simple, to wait for my board results and then get into university. But until then, I needed a job to survive. The first few days in the city were filled with bland bread and long walks. I would walk for several kilometers and stop at random shops, asking for a job. Amidst all this mess, I found happiness. I found myself wearing a saree in the window reflection. It was a rather unfamiliar experience for me, but I could see the beauty of the saree, and I admired it. I grew up dreaming of dressing in a saree as a symbol of maturity and power. When I moved to Mumbai, I bought a few sarees. This was to make myself look more mature and give myself the most probable chance of getting a job. I always told people I was 23 years old, even though I was a few years younger. Wearing a saree made me feel confident, empowered and proud."

She walked slowly forward, her feet barely touching the ground. She took a seat at the curb, and everything around her suddenly felt still. The air was quiet, almost mourning the absence of her sound for those few seconds.

"I met men of all ages, but their eyes were the same. I would often feel the stare on me, mostly around my waistline or backline. I would be scared to run away from them, not make eye contact. But ironically, after six months I fell in love with a handsome man."

I lit another cigarette for the night, watching her from a distance. I didn't want to interrupt her, or disturb the peace of the night, so I stayed where I was and watched her from afar.

"I found a job in a boutique and Pranav picked me up every night. It was a time when we would drive around the city, laugh with a cup of tea in a small tea stall, go to the movies, and rub our feet with love, and then our lust took over in the evening. At that moment, I realized the true beauty of sex. It was as if I had been taken to another plane of existence, a spiritual awakening of sorts. When two bodies come close and their skin touches, when their torsos move in unison with the intensity of the moment, it was as if two souls had become one. All of his was mine and all of mine was his. My hair would be spread out on the floor, and he would lie on my stomach. His body was like a furnace, radiating heat and filling me with warmth. From the scorching summer of May to the chilling winter of December, we experienced this deep desire. We lived like a married couple without arrangements or holy rituals."

Her silhouette was cast in the darkness surrounding her. Her face was serene and her hands lay lightly on her crossed legs. She seemed almost frozen in time and the shadows made her look like a goddess, an ideal image of grace and courage.

"I became pregnant that year. He was with me by my side for the first six months but then he had to leave for some place in the north for work. But he would call me every day and enquire about the baby. He was adamant that I quit my job and offered to cover all my expenses. We were so in love that we decided to get married once he returned. And one fine morning, I experienced my labor pain. I still remember that afternoon where I felt the pain as I walked towards the kitchen and screamed out of my lungs. There was no one around me when I walked into the lobby shouting for help. The last thing I remember was rolling down a staircase and seeing my blood dripping down several stairs like a waterfall."

She gently opened the car door and stepped in. Her eyes glazed over and her movements were dreamlike. I could see she was in a trance-like state, so I said nothing and started the engine. We drove down the winding cliff roads in silence, and I glanced over, her eyes firmly fixed ahead of her.

"The following morning, I heard that the baby had died. After closing all procedures, I walked out of the hospital. I was lost in my thoughts when I saw a huge billboard with a napkin ad on it. It brought me back to the reality of carrying a baby in my womb for ten months and the sorrow of losing it. The pain of that loss overwhelmed me and I started to cry on the pavement. Suddenly, three men walked up to me and introduced themselves as Pranav's friends. They said he had a terrible accident on his way to see me. And my life was again filled with darkness for several days."

XV

The car was filled with strange, almost oppressive silence until we reached the bottom of the cliff. She suddenly declared that she felt like eating something, prompting me to stop at a nearby diner. She put her chin on the window's surface and admired the deep blue sky. The moon slowly vanished behind huge clouds that seemed like a devil's silhouette. I drove slowly, admiring her hair as it flew towards me in the wild wind. What struck me in that moment was that she looked so different to my eyes. She shared all her stories smiling. The sorrow and tears she had hours ago at the metro seemed to be from a different person entirely. In a way, it was as if she wept to the mountains, and they listened to her. They took her worries away and left her with an emptiness that she would soon fill with joy and wonder.

Her sound continued to evolve, like a whisper in the wind. "I felt a chill on my skin and unbearable hunger as I slowly opened my eyes. Looking around, I noticed that the room I was in was a storeroom filled with broken wash basins, some pipes, a three-legged table, and a few drums. The atmosphere in the room was unpleasant. The dull red light hanging from the ceiling made it even more eerie.

I could hear the rain pouring outside, but there was no window to breathe fresh air. God, I remember every detail of this. I desperately searched for something to cover my body. Then I suddenly realized how long I had been lying there naked. The thought haunted me. Suddenly, I heard footsteps and a woman walked into the room, followed by men. I still remember the malicious grin on her face that day, as the group walked away. Afterwards, I was raped by several men from morning till night for the next week, during which they offered me food. I lay there, helpless and completely exposed, just like a dog tied outside a house."

"Who are these people?" I asked her in fear and anger. I found it difficult to focus on the road as I was overwhelmed by the emotion.

"I was completely taken aback by the lady's warning - she made it clear that if I didn't accept my future, the torture would continue. After that, they gave me some fancy clothes and one night, I was taken to a street with a man's company. I was asked to stand at the corner of a street. In the next few minutes, he walked out of the car, checking if anyone was looking at us. I wondered what he was about to do and felt my stomach tighten as my thoughts raced when he punched. He then grabbed my face and ordered me to dance, like a whore. And that night, I was picked up by a yellow car. The guy inside had all kinds of evil desires, and once he finished, I stumbled into the bathroom, feeling anger and despair. I bit my tongue, wishing for a quick death. Looking at myself in the mirror, I couldn't believe what I had become. The next day the woman gave me a new name and they all laughed uproariously at me for my first job I had completed for them as their whore. I wonder whether it was Pranav who played all these games with what I have become, treating me as his mere lab rat to experiment with all my sexual desires. My heart silently hates him but denies accepting the fact. And sometimes, it's better if a few things in life are left unanswered." She touched my hand, which rested on the gear, and gave a gentle smile while looking directly into my eyes.

Afterwards, we decided to halt at a quaint, late-night hotel to grab a bite to eat. The woman was busy making hot omelets and fresh dosas, so we ordered some. The place was filled with truck drivers and friendly dogs wandering between the tables, their tails wagging. The smell of the omelets was too tempting to resist, and soon we had a delicious meal in front of us.

"Simran said you're a writer, so if you write my story I don't want you to make me look like a depressed person. Fill my life with happiness and laughter!"

I smiled at her words.

"Where do you plan on heading next?" I asked, curious about her destination.

She paused for a moment before responding and saying, "To a safe place. It may not be the paradise I dream of, but it's planned and full of hope."

I understood that she didn't want to give me any details, but I felt curious about her future plans. Her past was a mystery to me, and her future was a blank slate.

"Right now, I feel like I am in a dream. When I wake up tomorrow, I will be far away. Amidst icy mountains, new possibilities await me. I am aware that the mountains will not desire me to carry my past along. What is taking place in my life right now and all that has happened to me in the past is nothing more than a memory. You, too, are part of my past now."

She smiled and I immediately felt a connection, like I was part of her family. I felt comforted by her presence, like I was surrounded by warmth I had never been touched before.

"I want you to think of me as a dream, an angel walking through your mind, a figment of your imagination that can't be real. When you wake up tomorrow, I will be gone."

It was something she was looking at that I wasn't sure about while she gazed up through the dense trees. Pointing up, she said, "Do you see that kite up there? I wish I could be like it, free and unbound, soaring through the sky, untethered by any kind of string."

After a moment, she added dreamily, "I want to fly anywhere I want, without a care in the world."

We finished our dinner and walked into the car. I said, "So I will remember you as Kite. That's your name."

We laughed even harder at the thought of Kite being her name.

"Kate," She thought, contemplating the name. "I've heard it before, I think. Was it an actress?" She wondered, trying to remember the name. She shrugged off, deciding it was a good name regardless. Perhaps it would be her new name.

"Or you are Kitess, like the princess you are about to become. Or a lioness for your courage. Kite lioness... Or Kate lioness... Kateness..."

"That's not even a name!" She exclaimed.

We laughed, the sound echoing in the silent car. We laughed until we cried and joked around until our sides hurt.

"What is your name?" she asked. After several hours of togetherness, we introduced ourselves.

"That's another funny story," I said with excitement. "My real name is twenty two characters long. Can you believe it?" I asked with a smile, shaking my head in disbelief.

"No way!" She gasped in surprise. "That's a lie!" Her eyes widened in amazement, her mouth agape in shock.

I said, "Yeah. I didn't like the name I had originally and decided to name myself after one of my favorite writers, Charles Bukowski. But then I thought, 'Bukowski isn't really an Indian name.' So, I settled on Charles. Later, an astrologer suggested that the name 'Charlie' would bring me luck in my career. I was young and impressionable, so I decided to stick with it and introduce myself as Charlie to everyone."

She turned to me and asked, "So did it bring you any luck?" The morning sun shone brightly through the windows, and the rush of air filling the car was invigorating.

"I have become a complete failure since that day. The hills we visited now, that was where he lived. I drove here seven years ago to grab his collar and smash his face. But when I got there, he was already dead and there was no trace of him anywhere. People said he was a conman."

The sound of her laughter filling the room was infectious. Tears of joy streamed down her temples as she could no longer contain her excitement. I simply stared at her for a moment, taking in the beauty before joining in her laughter. We laughed together for an eternity, both unable to control ourselves.

That morning, I dropped her off at the airport and watched her vanish through the huge windows like an angel. She never looked back, remaining a dream for the rest of my life. As I continued my journey, our joyous conversation lingered in my empty car. The exuberance and heartache that had filled the night, now extinct, leaving behind a solemn quiet. She was a presence that never faded.

That morning, I waved one last time, saying a final goodbye to my good friend, Kate.

XVI

The rehearsals concluded by five in the evening, and everyone gathered in a restaurant located between the beach and their theater to discuss plans for the big day. Bejoy, in high spirits, treated the entire crew to a bar. He requested the waiter to join three tables so that all his team members could sit together. He had never seen such a tremendous response to their show's registration at his theater, and he was elated. On their way to the beach, he kept expressing gratitude and excitement to Apu for making this event a success. Bejoy was certain that this show would bring fame to the theater and ensure its continued success.

Apu sat between Bejoy and Maya, feeling overwhelmed by Bejoy's hospitality. The table was filled with various seafood dishes, but as a vegetarian since his marriage to Farhaan, Apu ordered himself a vegetarian pizza. He was grateful to Farhaan for introducing him to vegetarianism.

"I am ecstatic about the numbers. Can you believe it? We have a total of 98 entries. Last time, there were only 8 of us when we performed," Bejoy continued, beaming with excitement as they awaited their drinks.

Maya exclaimed, "Wow, that's an impressive number! Our theater has never seen such a response over the years. And all the credit goes to the man of the hour, Apu!" The open restaurant erupted with applause, as if in agreement with Maya.

Bejoy gestured towards Apu as if presenting him to the entire group and said, "All credit goes to our teacher, mentor, and the greatest actor." Apu greeted them with a warm smile and thanked everyone humbly. The claps reverberated along with the soothing sound of the nearby beach, drawing the attention of some guests from the restaurant.

The table was soon filled with food and drinks. Bejoy urged Apu to have a drink, but Apu politely declined.

"I never thought I would be eating with huge vaginas, penises, and pubic hairs next to me," Maya exclaimed with a mix of amusement and surprise. They had cardboard cutouts of various shapes—vaginas, penises, and pubic hairs—which Bejoy had brought from the theater to add some artistic flair to the table.

Paul, another theater artist from their team, playfully placed a piece of black-dyed cotton, resembling pubic hair, on Maya's plate, teasing her, "You're about to eat a vagina now."

"You're sick! So damn sick!" Maya retaliated, chasing Paul across the restaurant with a cardboard penis in her hand, nearly four feet long. Laughter filled the air as she mockingly threatened Paul.

Suddenly, a man from the next table recognized Apu and yelled, "Hey, there's our anal fucker!" Apu panicked as he looked at them, but the man quickly pointed to his friend, pretending the comment wasn't directed at Apu. The other friend hissed "ussss...", which is considered as a derogatory term for a transgender person.

Apu swallowed hard, and the table fell into an uncomfortable silence. The team pretended not to have heard anything and focused on their food.

Bejoy decided to break the silence and asked Apu, "Where are you heading next?"

Apu wiped his lips with a cloth and replied, "First, I'm going back to Mumbai to see my daughter. I have been contacted by two theater houses there, so I will be joining them after a short break. I have also signed up for an online masterclass on acting with an old friend. I'll be keeping busy with that."

"Sounds interesting. When will you visit Kerala again?" Bejoy inquired.

"Whenever you invite me again," Apu responded, drawing smiles from everyone at the table.

Maya moved closer to Apu, captivated by his energetic smile. She then spoke, "Your lesson yesterday about observing human emotions helped me gain a new perspective on life."

"Excellent! How did it go?" Apu felt thrilled that his experiment had proven successful.

"I didn't take a bus or sit in a park. Just across the street, as I was heading towards the bus stop, I watched an old man standing in the corner, smiling at something in front of him." She sipped her beer.

"So, what was so special about it?" Apu asked as he enjoyed a piece of pizza.

"He was blind, Apu. Across from him, there was an open ground where people littered, buffaloes lazed about, kids played volleyball, and two men were drying clothes, hanging them on a string. All the clothes were white, creating the impression that the attire, the ground, and the men themselves belonged to some hotel. But I couldn't help but wonder what had brought that smile to the old man's face," Maya explained, attempting to recollect every detail of the moment.

"Did you ask him?" Apu glanced around the table at their friends who were engrossed in laughter and indulging in the food. Then he turned his attention back to Maya, eager to hear the story she had observed.

"Yes, I did. At first, he seemed surprised to hear a voice. He nodded unsteadily in the direction of my voice and remained silent for a few moments. The old man continued to gaze straight at the drying clothes. After a while, he shared that he was thinking about his late wife. The scent of the detergent had reminded him of the time he had spent with her before she passed away from Alzheimer's. As we walked away from there, he apologized to me for not responding immediately, explaining that he didn't want to lose himself in the moment because it felt so alive. We ended up going to lunch together."

Maya snapped out of her trance-like state and reached for a slice of pizza from Apu, and they exchanged a warm smile. As the evening progressed, the team continued to order drinks, gradually letting loose. Apu ordered a Pepsi for himself and seized the opportunity to have a conversation with Bejoy.

"Hey, listen. I want to talk to you about something," Apu said.

"Sure, let's go out for a smoke. Do you mind joining me?" Bejoy suggested.

They walked out of the restaurant and sat on the beach sand.

"It wasn't right, what happened there," Bejoy said as he sipped his beer.

"What wasn't right?" Apu asked.

"The men and what they said," Bejoy replied.

"It's okay. We can't control what everyone says. Besides, no matter how far you try to run from your past or change yourself, it will always be a part of you, like an annoying piece of gum stuck to your shoe. Those boys were just confused between a transgender person and a gay person. Maybe they should watch our play to improve their sex education," Apu chuckled.

Bejoy smiled and said, "Yeah, maybe they should."

"You sure you don't want a cigarette?" Bejoy offered Apu his cigarette box.

Apu declined with a shake of his head, saying, "Trust me, my body has had enough cigarettes and whisky to last a lifetime. Sometimes, I feel like it's all saved up, like I am a barrel and I can get high just by thinking about it."

"I get it. Being an actor isn't as easy as it looks. I have friends in the industry, and I know it can be tough sometimes." Bejoy took a drag from his cigarette.

"Yeah... yeah... I was thinking that... we should include a Kathakali play tomorrow with our other shows. What do you think?" Apu proposed.

Bejoy exhaled a long puff of smoke into the beach air and pondered for a while before responding, "Man, I know you are a great artist. But this idea... I don't think it's a good one. You know what kind of audience we are targeting, right? Mostly youngsters. I believe this might change the context."

"No, it will definitely work. You gotta trust me on this," Apu insisted.

"I do trust you. But we are putting on an erotic show. The idea is to talk about sex... address menstruation problems... and explore coming-of-age themes. It's about breaking taboos and encouraging open conversations. How do you think Kathakali fits into this play?"

Apu couldn't think of an immediate answer, but he was determined to convince Bejoy to accept his suggestion. "We can make it our grand finale. A compliment to the audience, like saying thanks in a cultured way," Apu said earnestly.

"What is this, serving complimentary food to the audience?" Bejoy teased as he headed inside the restaurant. "Even if you give it as a compliment, where will you find a Kathakali artist in just two days?" He then asked skeptically.

Apu folded his hands close to his chest and stood in front of him. After they both exchanged perplexed looks, Apu slowly pointed his index finger at himself.

"No way. When was the last time you performed this art? This is not something that can be pulled off overnight," Bejoy said, still unsure.

After thinking for a while, Apu wanted to organize his thoughts and find the right words to convey to Bejoy. Then, with confidence, Apu replied. "If you don't eat food for a month, will you forget how to eat?"

"What is your point here?" Bejoy was still confused.

"That's how this art is for me. My father taught me this art when I was 5, and I have been performing or observing it ever since. This means a lot to me, and performing it in the land where I was born is something special. Please, let me do this. Let me take care of it," Apu implored.

"What's the story?"

"I don't know... I mean... I will figure it out."

Bejoy checked his watch and said, perplexed, "Figure it out? We hardly have 40 hours for the show, and you haven't done this in over 20 years. How are you going to do it?"

"All I want you to do is trust me. Because I trust myself. This art is within me, like it is a part of my soul, and I know it... I can feel it... And if things don't go well, you can have my money. You don't need to pay me anything," Apu assured him.

Bejoy leered at Apu for a while, and said, "God, I need another cigarette." He walked out again.

Apu's face lit up with excitement as he thanked Bejoy.

XVII

I woke up in a single cart bed, my mind still foggy from the nightmare I had. Trying to remember where I was, I glanced at the clock to calculate how long I had been sleeping. My hair had been completely matted down from the pillow, and I could feel sticky saliva around my lips. After driving for an entire day, exhaustion has taken its toll. However, I had managed only four hours of sleep, yet it felt as if I had been slumbering for days.

Nights are a special kind of torture for me and nightmares are the main reason I struggle to get a good night's sleep. As soon as the sun sets, my heart races and my mind floods with anxious thoughts. I lay down in bed, trying to find a comfortable position, but it's never enough. Some nights, I try to write down the stories that haunt me, only to get stuck in the same scene, unable to move forward. Other nights, I imagine I'm painting the forests of my dreams in my mind's eye, and I almost feel like I'm there. Then there are those nights when I'm so restless and my mind is so active that I feel like running a marathon.

The thoughts swirling around in my head seemed incomprehensible. I wrote until early in the morning and when I put my pen down, I knew I would tear out these pages and throw them away, never wanting to see them again.

I stepped through the door, the cool night air brushing against my skin. It looked as if the tree branches danced in the moonlight against the dark sky. A soft drizzle filled the sky, painting a beautiful gray canvas. I lit the cigarette and the nicotine soothed my chest ache. Taking a deep breath, I realized that I had followed the address Kate had left on her seat before she departed from the car. The address led me to Thrissur, Kerala. I then let the gentle Kerala breeze caress me. This reminded me that it had been a day since I left Kate at the airport.

I tried to remember what happened the night before when I met Yaqoob and he handed me the keys to this room. It was dark and late, so I couldn't see his face. His house was next to mine, and it felt strange to think a family lived in a graveyard.

The cigarette smoke hung low in the air, slowly absorbed by the gentle rain. I tried to piece together the visuals from the nightmare I had just woken up from. It was a strange dream, one I couldn't understand. I tried to recall the details, sights and sounds. It felt like two distinct realities intertwined, with only a few scenes clear in my mind. I stared into the darkness, focusing my energy on the dream, and gradually the images became sharper.

I was sitting in a car in my first dream, though it didn't feel like mine. It was parked at the edge of a mountain covered with small green grass blades. The landscape in front of me was filled with magnificent buildings. It was a beautiful sight, and I was mesmerized by the scenery. I felt relaxed, as if I had been in this place for a long time. The car felt like a sanctuary, and I was content to stay and enjoy the view. I slowly turned to my left, leaned closer and kissed.

The person's face was an enigma, shrouded in bandages, with only a small hollow opening at the mouth. In the midst of our passionate kiss, I noticed that the lips and skin were rough, as if they had been recently shaved.

The world was burning right in front of my eyes, yet there was no sound to be heard. It was as if the world had been attacked by a nuclear weapon. Buildings collapsed and erupted in massive gray smoke. However, the air inside the car was so still that it seemed like neither of us were part of this chaotic scene. All I could focus on were the lips of the person sitting next to me. I couldn't see much else, but I could tell it was a man.

I exhaled a deep puff of smoke as my dream pictures played out before my eyes. The weight of the dream was heavy, and I couldn't shake the feeling of unease it left me with. I lit another cigarette, trying to focus my attention on the other dream I had experienced. This dream felt different from the last, more tangible and more real.

It was a long road, lined with vast farmlands on either side. Not a single building was in sight, and yet the scenery was captivating; wheat fields, a wide muddy road, and the vast expanse of a clear blue sky. It was like a painting, still and silent. No human presence, no animals, just unearthly silence. The man quickly scrambled to his feet, clutching the papers to his chest. He looked confused and tired, with sweat beads on his forehead. He glanced around, his eyes searching for the source of the noise. Was it coming from me? I couldn't be sure. The sound of a large crowd grew louder and closer, as if they were running towards me. The man, or maybe it was me, seemed terrified, desperately trying to locate the noise source. I was frozen in fear, unable to move. In this moment, I realized it was my own body that felt foreign to me.

I was taken aback by its suddenness. One moment I was standing still in silence, the next the ground shook with the sound of thousands of footsteps running towards me. I had no choice but to join in the stampede, pushing my legs to keep up with the intense pace. It felt like we were all on the final lap of a marathon. The prize was something we all wanted and desperately needed, yet remained unknown.

The road ahead of us split in two, with everyone continuing to the left. I had to use all my strength to keep up while also keeping a firm grip on the papers I was holding. I tried to get out of the crowd, feeling like I was choking on the stifling mass of people. Everyone ran together in the same direction, like a herd of wild buffaloes. Suddenly, a man pushed me down and I was stamped over by a crowd. But even as I lay there, I couldn't help but stare up at the empty road ahead of me. This was visible between the legs of the people sprinting by. I had to leave, no matter what. As I slowly turned over, there were several men like me being trampled, trying to crawl out of the crowd. Suddenly, as one last man stepped over me in a hurry, the mud beneath me sucked me down. I felt myself falling through an abyss of darkness, my body covered in blood.

***

The eerie silence of the early morning was broken only by pouring rain. The asbestos on the roof of my room seemed to amplify it, as if spirits from the grave called me into their world. I knew I wouldn't be able to sleep after this nightmare, so I decided to walk into the unknown.

I took a deep breath as I stepped out into the rain. The light drizzle felt refreshing against my skin, tousling my hair as I stood in the open. The rain was slowing as the sun emerged from the gray clouds, its yellow rays spreading slowly like a bird hatching from its egg. Yaqoob walked out of his house and I could tell from his back that he gave me the keys last night. His wife also stepped out of the house, and it seemed like they were getting ready for morning prayer.

I followed him as he walked between the graves, jumped into a pit and pushed the mud aside. He was a young man with a slim figure and a patchy beard. His head was wrapped in a blue towel and he wore a stained vest and lungi. He nodded his head in greeting when he saw me walking towards him, and I waved back awkwardly. It was a strange thought to consider that a young man was entrusted with such significant responsibility—to take care of a graveyard, where many bodies were peacefully resting, under his watchful eye.

He slowly pulled himself up from the mud-filled pit, his body covered in thick, wet substance. I looked at the grave and asked him if it was for me? He shook his head and said no. He pushed the mud from his body, dirt clumps falling to the ground. His face seemed familiar, a part of me recognized him even though I couldn't place from where.

He walked away with a murmur, "Yours will be ready by night." His rush implied a sense of arrogance as he hurried away.

I stood there, in the middle of the vast graveyard, surrounded by an unsettling silence. Every grave was the same size, no matter the differences between the bodies buried within them. There was no distinction between the rich and the poor, the young and the old, the businessman and the laborer, the rapist and the thief, the scholar and the gay, the crippled and everyone else. It felt like a huge scam, a world in which we all live with different beliefs, running our lives trusting in something intangible and often beyond our understanding. We devote so much of our time and energy to the afterlife, that we forget to take pleasure from the present moment. In the end, we are all just bones mixed with mud. Are these bones tall enough to reach the heavens? I shrugged without an answer.

I have spent my entire life asking questions about my existence. I look up to the sky and speak, without addressing anyone in particular, "Why I was brought into this world and what my purpose could be among millions of others." It felt like the graveyard whispered answers to me, though I'm not sure exactly what it's trying to tell. I felt like I was on the cusp of discovering something profound, but I could never quite put my finger on it.

Life seemed like a huge stage play to me on that day. We rehearsed for months, perfecting our lines and movements. When the curtains open, we are ready to entertain the huge audience in front of us. We give it our all, giving our highest quality of performance. And when the curtains close, we are tired and get back to our true selves. We jump into our beds at night, hopeful for the next day and a fresh episode.

My hands instinctively reached for my pocket and I pulled out a cigarette. I was about to light it when I heard Yaqoob's voice ring out. He stood there, washing the dirt off his clothes, a small figure in front of the grand mosque.

"I respect the dead. Please come out. Do not smoke there." His voice reverberated through the vast graveyard, echoing off the trees and awakening the dead.

I waved my hand to show him that I wasn't going to smoke in the graveyard. I walked away, trying to find the way out of there, keeping an eye out for the exit.

***

I walked through the massive mosque walls and leaned against my car parked at the entrance. All around me, the call for morning prayer reverberated through the speakers.

This signaled to the city's Muslims to wake up and come for prayer. The sky was a breathtaking mix of blues, yellows, and pinks, and I could see small, energetic birds flitting around. I breathed deeply, absorbing the peaceful atmosphere.

A slim figure passed me by wearing a cape tied around her neck, fluttering behind her. She was young, with cropped hair, and while her mannerisms and clothing were those of a boy, her soft skin revealed she was a girl. She had an unusual style. The girl wore loose baggy pants and a black t-shirt. However, the cape she wore over it was a deep, proud color that was unmistakable.

I could hear her wheezing as she walked down the street. She had taken heavy steps and tried to hail an auto rickshaw, but they all ignored her. Standing there for a few moments, she shouted out to me from the corner of the street. She asked if I could give her a ride. My mind was still wavering about the dream I had earlier, but she drew me like a magnet. Without thinking twice, I nodded and dropped my cigarette.

She hopped into my car, gently laying her cape on her lap. As I asked about our destination, she replied to a place I hadn't heard of before. When I mentioned that this place was new for me, she said she would guide me along the route. We drove for about fifteen minutes, during which we hardly spoke. Yet, her joy was evident in the way she enjoyed the morning breeze brushing her face as she hummed a song. It seemed like she was taking in the beauty of the world around her.

I felt a sense of stupor when we pulled the car up to the corner of the massive ground. It almost seemed like a sprawling open city, with its own unique culture and energy. Everywhere I looked, the place was filled with colors of the same flag proudly displayed by individuals in some way or another. The place's atmosphere was electric, and I couldn't help but be drawn in by its vibrancy. I felt a strong connection to this place and the people within it. It was clear that I had stumbled upon something truly special.

She snapped me out of my thoughts and said, "You look like my father."

She kept her eyes fixed on my face, searching for something I couldn't define. My throat tightened and my mouth dried, as I swallowed, unsure of how to respond at that moment.

"Do you mind if I add something to your face? You have an alluring structure."

I looked into the rear mirror and saw my huge face staring back. It was like thick, oiled skin stretched over a round ball, with a gray beard and my messy hair pulled up. I adjusted my huge black spectacles, wondering what she found attractive about my face.

As I turned towards her, she held my chin gracefully and asked me to close my eyes. Her energy passed me well, and I tried to be in the moment as she suggested. The bottom of my nose was tingling with a heavy sensation. Beneath the darkness of my eyes shut, I could hear her asking me not to open my eyes until she approved. I heard a rustling sound, like she was searching for something in her bag.

"Now!" she said.

My eyes widened as I looked into the oval shaped wooden framed mirror she held in front of me. A clipped nose ring dangled from my nose and touched my chin. It was a huge, circular ring that sparkled in the light. I was mesmerized by it, and felt like I could see into my future.

"It's my ear ring, but it looks nice on your face." I watched as she lightly tapped my nose and walked away from the car, carrying the mirror with her.

I could feel my face stretching while looking at my reflection in the rearview mirror. I was trying to get used to this new piece of jewelry on my face and briefly caught sight of her figure through the windshield, walking slowly and carefully to cross the road.

"How do I smoke a cigarette with this hanging here?" I shouted out of my car window.

"You can place your cigarette there and give some rest to your fingers. It looks like an innovation and you look cool with it."

She shouted back in response. A giggle escaped her lips as she walked into the crowd.

***

A pang of jealousy and a gust of happiness rushed inside me as I watched the crowd grow exponentially from inside my car. Smiles and laughter filled the massive ground. They wore pride colors on sign boards, t-shirts, flags, and capes. Everyone seemed in good spirits as they eagerly waited for the rally to begin. I admired the overwhelming energy and enthusiasm brought to the venue.

I stepped out of the car and joined the crowd. Everywhere I looked, it was full of life. Dozens of stalls lined the streets, selling badges and other trinkets, and people bustled around, chatter filling the air. Further down, I spotted a lesbian couple who had set up a stand, offering free omelets and sandwiches as breakfast for the crowd. The couple's infectious smile was the cherry on top. The warm, delicious aroma of the omelets was tantalizing and made my mouth water. I greeted them shyly, my awkwardness palpable, and looked at the huge oil drums they used as a stand to fry their omelets. I delicately pulled the nose ring out of my face, feeling discomfort as I did so.

As I sat eating, I observed the humans in the room. They all seemed interesting in their own way, and I was enchanted by their presence. Some were talking, some laughed, and some quietly walked carefree. It felt like I was in a different world, a world where judgment didn't exist and everyone accepted each other's flaws. The crowd had an air of positivity around them, and I soaked it in. I felt free and liberated, like I could do or be whatever I wanted without fear of judgment.

I noticed a gay couple strolling together, holding hands and casually kissing. I was taken aback by the sight, as I had never seen something like this before. However, I continued on my way, and in a nearby circle, I saw the girl I had just dropped off seated among other vibrant people under a towering tree. As I walked closer to the circle, I saw a trans woman finishing a speech. The audience applauded and cheered.

Dozens of people were sitting in a circle, all with beaming smiles and contentment in their eyes. The atmosphere was so inviting, and spread with a sense of community and togetherness radiating from the group. I noticed that the circle center was left open for others to join in and share their stories. Few groups of people were deep in discussion and welcomed the next person to join them. They pulled him in with laughter and brought him to the center of the group. He walked back to place his shoulder bag on the chair. As I tried to get a better look at him, the girl I had just dropped off located me in the crowd. She waved at me with her mouth wide open in excitement. I waved back at her and looked at the man.

He had a gentle, peaceful demeanor that put everyone at ease. His silver eyes had a spark of intelligence and his voice was deep and soothing. He wore a beige T-shirt with a proud badge pinned to his chest. As my gaze collected a clear vision of him, I felt my heart race and sink into my seat.

The man clasped his hands tightly and his eyes flitted through the crowd before speaking. His lips curved slightly, a small smile playing at the edges, as if his words were ready and eager to pour out with joy.

"I am recognized by my stage name, the thick name you have seen on posters. But that's not my real name. And people here, people who know who I am are familiar with my name. So to people who don't know my real name, I am Apu and I am a theater artist now and not a hero." He brought his fingers together in a gesture of emphasis as he quoted those words.

"When did you first fall in love?" He asked a boy in the front row. The boy replied 18.

"Good age." He nodded. "I fell in love when I was 20 years old... when I moved to Mumbai." Apu stopped, his mouth half-opened as he tried to arrange his thoughts in a meaningful way. He spoke slowly, allowing his words to linger in the air and settle into the scene.

"I still remember the first time I saw him. He used to sit in the corner of our room and there was a window very close to him. He would use this place to throw away his cigarette buds and crumbled writings which he hated." He smiled as he walked into the past.

"I stayed in my friend's room. He worked as an assistant director then. He would say that everyone would fear this guy sitting next to the window, because sometimes he might become hyper and arrogant. So I was scared at first, but my eyes automatically drifted towards him. And when he looks at me, I would turn away with my heart pounding."

Apu glanced around the place, seeing the new group of people gathered, their faces alive with excitement. He could tell that they were eager to hear his story, and he gave them a cordial nod in greeting.

"I would stroll around the city seeking opportunity as an actor and when I returned home, my place would be opposite his, and the exchange of looks continued. After a few days, he would stare at me all day and scribble on his papers and sometimes throw them aggressively through the window. I felt like I was an art model and he was an artist, trying to capture my likeness on canvas. I enjoyed the room's atmosphere. I could have happily remained there, still and silent, allowing him to observe me and write whatever he felt like."

"Did he look cute?" One guy shouted from the stands and the crowd laughed.

"No! He looked like he would eat me whole. But I liked him as he was. He was huge with a big tummy and hair covered his body. And I was very thin back then."

He paused for a moment, needing a drink of water. Searching around, he saw a young girl standing nearby, and he asked her if she could lend him a water bottle.

"One day when I woke up he was all dressed and waiting near my face for me to open my eyes. He asked me to get ready and meet someone. Later that day he took me to a director and yes, he was the writer of my first film. I didn't know what he was writing or how he knew this director. However, he looked hungry to see me act in front of those cameras and give birth to his story." As his voice echoed through the air, the crowd sparkled with wonder.

"During this shooting time, I felt low most of the days. I was so lucky to have him, my only support, there for me. He shared his wisdom and pushed me to become an actor. His unwavering dedication to helping me reach my dreams was apparent, and I saw the feelings he had for me in his every action. And during these days, I realized I fell in love with him."

He took a few sips of water from the bottle.

"The film was released and was a blockbuster hit. Everyone was fascinated by his story and my acting and we became the talk of the town. The film unit attended many events but he didn't appear. But, he was there for one event and I felt a deep emotion for not seeing him for a long time. That day we were presented with a watch, a Rado. As he was standing by my side I started feeling an uncontrollable emotion that I had sealed in for him. Out of control, I tried to hold his hand when we were applauded by the crowd in front of us. He pushed my hands away and scowled at me."

Taking a deep breath, he spoke excruciatingly. This was almost as if each word had to be carefully chosen and placed to convey his gravity.

"I felt an overwhelming sense of anguish as I entered my bedroom that night. Standing in front of the mirror, I slowly undressed. My hands trembled as I removed each piece of clothing. The pain inside me grew with each step. I was curled up in a small ball, feeling weak and helpless. My heart pounded as he burst into the room, taking me by surprise. He leapt onto the bed and grabbed me, lifting me up and throwing me onto the floor. A punch to my face followed, smashing my nose and breaking my jaw. I lay there, letting him slam all his anger to my face with infinite punches. Tears filled at the edge of his eyes, struggling to be released. Just like him, it felt like these emotions were sealed away, hidden from the world. I knew he loved me all this time."

Apu gazed into the abyss. When he forcefully distracted himself, he scanned the crowd in front of him. Gradually, a smile crept across his face.

"Love is like cigarette smoke. It spirals its way through the air, yet if one holds onto it too tightly, they will choke. That was the last time I saw him. After he left the room, I sank myself into the bathtub and wanted to start over as a new man. But I became drunk, an alcoholic, and after a few successful hits, I became a failure with controversy."

His eyes suddenly sparkled and joy filled his face.

"But that's when I met my husband. My sorrow was lifted by another soul, letting me walk into this light. Who gave me the opportunity to become a proud husband and father. But I would still tell him that you will be my husband, but this writer will always be my first love." He chuckled and the crowd smiled in response

"But nobody should ever let their identity be defined by society's expectations. You are a strength to this society, not a source of shame. Let us all take a stand and spread love instead. And we shall all have the strength to accept who we are and understand our bodies."

Apu's words resonated deeply with the audience, his voice erupted with emotion, and the crowd rose to its feet, clapping and cheering for him. He bowed to them in thanks, the applause continuing until he took his seat.

I waited there, among the throng of people, for him to sit and eventually he did. Taking this as my cue, I rose from my seat and left the crowd. The noise of people slowly faded away behind me.

I sat in my car and watched the crowd, feeling home and comfort. My heart wanted to stay, yet I also didn't want Apu to see me. After a few moments, I decided to move my car to a spot further away. This was so I could be hidden from view, yet still stay and observe the people around me.

I lay in my car, enveloped in solitude. My mind was stroked by a glimpse of the past. The blue room I shared with Apu twenty years prior looked vivid in front of me as if we had lived there yesterday. The walls were painted blue, with only the slightest hint of another hue here and there. The room was small, barely ten by ten feet, but it seemed huge. Despite sitting opposite each other, we felt miles apart. I wondered where he had been all these years, yet I still felt close to him in my heart. The thought of my grave being dug crossed my mind between thoughts. The joy I had experienced during the last two days before my death seemed like a blessing. With that blessing I drove back to the graveyard. The emotions that flooded my heart were a mix of sadness and acceptance.

As I looked fixedly out into the vast emptiness, I was struck by another strange thought. I realized that I write when I am in pain. Some people turn to drinking, some find solace in talking to their loved ones, while others express themselves through art. Music, cinema, and writing. Pain is a universal emotion experienced by everyone. Writing is a way for me to process my experiences and express my innermost feelings. And so, I want my writing to touch the soul, not just the lips. And pain, what kind of hurtful emotion is this? My conscience whispered. It's painful when we are in poverty, our midlife crisis is a disaster, or our friends leave us. But out of all of these, the pain caused by love is what we take most personally. It can break our hearts and shatter our souls, and the pain may even be permanent. Eventually, we may forget their appearance, but the thought of that person can become a habit. A part of that person living in our thoughts for eternity. But, when we die, will their thoughts still linger with us? Will we take their shared moments and memories to our graves? Would you still be able to write when you are dead and leave this world? I thought to myself, maybe I should wait for death and find out.

Glancing out of my car windshield, I realized that the day had flown by and the hours were quickly ticking away. I was driving at full speed when I noticed someone standing on the side of the road, trying to flag down a ride—it seemed that their car had broken down. Despite an urgent need for help, I kept driving, not wanting another passenger.

XVIII

Slowly, Apu made his way into the dressing room, completing his performance, and stood before the mirror. The orange bulbs surrounding the mirror cast a radiant glow, yet Apu found himself reluctant to remove his makeup. He yearned to immerse himself entirely in his character, seeking refuge within its embrace. Although he believed he had performed well, anxiety gnawed at him, wondering how the audience perceived his act. He even noticed some people leaving during his performance, adding to his unease. Nevertheless, when he finished, the audience erupted in applause, leaving him waiting anxiously for their feedback.

The car broke down on their way to the theater after leaving the rally. However, they finally managed to find a ride and reached the theater by afternoon. Unfortunately, the face paint artist bailed at the last moment, forcing Apu to relearn his skills and paint his own face. He hired a few other Kathakali artists from the neighboring village with the help of Bejoy, who would play along with him. Amidst the frenzied activity in the dressing room, Apu asked for a mirror of his own and patiently and meticulously layered his face with paint. The process began in the afternoon and persisted for five hours, even after the show began at seven in the evening. Despite his relentless efforts, Bejoy wasn't pleased with Apu's decision, fearing it would result in a chaotic outcome.

Apu decided to enact the same play he performed the last time he left his home. The play revolved around the story of "The Triumph of Virtue," which is a single-act Kathakali play that revolves around the clash between good and evil, embodied by Prince Vikram and the malevolent Demoness Maneka. Set against the backdrop of ancient India, the play explores themes of bravery, righteousness, and the power of virtue to overcome darkness. Their Kathakali performance weaved together expressive gestures, rhythmic footwork, and elaborate costumes to bring this timeless tale to life. In this play, Apu portrayed the role of the great Prince Vikram. He wore a traditional, brightly colored costume known as a 'Chutti.' Although it was difficult to get the exact costume at the last minute, he felt convinced with the one he found. It typically consists of a vibrant skirt, ornate waistbands, and a stylized, embroidered jacket called 'Chatta.' He painted his face with traditional green and yellow to depict the character, signifying his virtuous and noble nature. The green color symbolizes virtue and heroism, while yellow represents a divine aura.

As a child, Apu's brother, rather than his father, had taught him the art and knowledge of face painting. Nevertheless, Apu credited his father for nurturing his artistic talent. Wishing his brother could be there to witness his performance, he reluctantly pushed away the optimism, knowing it was unlikely. Standing before the mirror now, memories of the night he left his hometown resurfaced. The boy, who once attempted to rub off the makeup from his face and remove the costume hastily, now found himself two decades later surrendering to his character. He buried himself within the layers of this costume, embracing the role with all his heart and soul.

The crowd's enthusiasm still echoed from the distance as Apu heard their chatter about the other artists' speeches. But he remained fixated on his reflection in the mirror, the image reminding him of his last day as an actor.

He remembered stumbling out of his room one afternoon, intoxicated. Usually, his cook, Seetha akka will be preparing lunch in the kitchen while her baby plays in the living area. The television would be on, as Seetha akka loved to stay updated with the news. But that day, she was absent, leaving behind traces of her hurried departure—the baby's kerchief and the partially switched-off TV. Apu then went to the garden, searching for his gardener, Tenali, who also seemed to have left abruptly, leaving scattered trimmed bushes and the garden scissors lying unattended.

Disoriented and hungover, Apu made himself some black coffee and turned on the television, only to be met with a heartbreaking revelation. His face plastered on every news channel, reporters excitedly sharing stories about him, stories he was oblivious to. Pressing the remote to his lips to suppress his emotions, he eventually turned off the television and reached for his phone, discovering 96 missed calls, 14 of them from his lawyer. Trying to call back, he found his phone battery dead.

With a heavy heart, he stepped out of the house, bracing himself for whatever lay ahead. Seeking solace, he settled in the heart of his sprawling garden, a vast expanse capable of accommodating over 50 cars or welcoming more than 1000 guests. The property's rustic charm evoked memories of his hometown, a comforting reminder of simpler times.

Despite facing disapproval from all quarters over the audacious purchase of this property for twenty-four crores rupees, he had remained unwavering in his decision. After pouring himself a drink and setting the whisky bottle down by his side, he gazed pensively at the afternoon sky, feeling utterly lost. Half-hidden in the shed, his prized Lamborghini stood as a silent testament to past events. The front bonnet bore visible scars from an unfortunate incident that occurred while driving back home from the bar.

All his upcoming projects were canceled, and no director dared to sign him for over a year. The fame he had amassed from his string of successful films had vanished from the audience's memory. It was all temporary, shattered by a bitter feud with a leading producer in the industry.

Despite delivering consecutive hits, the producer signed him for a substantial sum for three films. Unfortunately, the first film bombed at the box office, prompting Apu to choose a different director with better content to recover the losses. The producer vehemently opposed this decision, leading to heated arguments that culminated in a physical altercation, halted only by the intervention of others. The producer vowed to destroy Apu's career, and he succeeded. He threatened directors and producers to avoid working with Apu and, later, uncovered his sexual orientation, intending to use it against him. Apu had always known that he was more attracted to men than women, but he feared that coming out would tarnish his image as a romantic actor and ruin his career. He had been entangled in a complicated and secret affair with his makeup man, a relationship that they both kept hidden from the prying eyes of the world. However, as whispers and gossip spread among the crew members, he felt the walls closing in around them. Fearing the consequences of their secret being exposed, he made the difficult decision to shut it off, putting an end to their clandestine love. He then attempted to maintain a relationship with a female co-star to preserve his image, but the struggle to hide his true self took a toll on him emotionally.

The producer manipulated the co-star, promising her a significant role in his next film in exchange for accusing Apu of inappropriate behavior involving their sexual life. Additionally, he coerced Apu's makeup artist into filing a harassment complaint against him. The producer even dug up records of financial discrepancies, falsely claiming that Apu had taken an advance payment without fulfilling his end of the bargain. With this concoction of allegations, the producer successfully cast Apu out of the industry, leaving him defeated.

Apu finally came to accept that he had lost the battle against the vindictive producer. Yet, he knew deep down that his true battle had always been with himself. Emotions swirling inside him, he reached for the whisky and glass, then made his way towards the colossal shards of broken glass that had once formed his wardrobe. Staring at his own reflection in the mirror, he was startled by the stranger that looked back at him. A man he hadn't truly seen in a long time—a pale, weak, and disillusioned version of his former self. Aversion gripped him as he confronted the man he had become, and all the emotions he had suppressed came pouring out. Tears streamed down his cheeks as he wept, releasing the pain and turmoil that had consumed him for far too long.

When Apu turned eight years old, his sister presented him with a huge gift box. The box was well wrapped with blue satin and a golden texture. It was so fancy that he curiously grabbed it from his sister, not even bothering to say thanks. The box was tightly wrapped, and he was too impatient to remove it neatly, so he put a hole in it and peeped inside. The box was empty and dark, shallow with cardboard on all sides. When his sister saw the disappointment in him, she gave him a chocolate. Apu thought he was like this box now—colorful outside and shallow inside. The next year, his sister died. The doctor said it was malaria, but he believed it was poverty that killed her.

He had chased after money, fame, and the adoration of countless fans, only to find that none of it brought him the satisfaction he had hoped for. The glossy banners and the applause of the masses felt hollow and meaningless in the face of his inner struggles. In that moment of profound realization, he understood that this wasn't the life he truly desired. With a surge of anger and liberation, he hurled the whisky bottle at the mirror, shattering it into countless fragments. The shards lay scattered around, reflecting the broken pieces of his soul. He then flung his glass onto the debris, signifying his decision to shatter the facade he had been upholding. Determined to take control of his life, he retreated into his room and dialed his lawyer's number. That day, Apu made a life-altering choice. He sold off everything he owned, severing the ties that bound him to the life of a glamorous star.

Standing in front of a different mirror now, he felt overwhelmed by what he had become. A flicker of hope arose, as Farhaan's words echoed in his mind.

"As we walk on this journey between life and death, we have to slice a part of our soul every day and leave it behind us. When there is nothing more to slice off, that is death. And if you could walk into another day, that is life. "

Apu's cheek muscles wiggled as he remained immersed in his character. Gracefully, he rotated by pushing his toes, returning to the position where he had stood before. With his hands brought close to his chest, he bowed before the mirror, expressing gratitude for everything that had happened to him.

Maya interrupted his solo show in front of the mirror and called him to the stage to thank the audience as they were closing the show. Apu replied with his eyes, winking multiple times while his hands remained bowed in front of the mirror. Blushing, Maya hurriedly returned to the stage. Apu slowly released himself from his posture and gently removed his crown.

As he made his way towards the stage, he reached for his phone and texted Farhaan, "Thanks for helping me find myself. Thanks for standing by my side when I was a mess. Thanks for redefining my life. Thanks for giving strength to my life and showing light when I was in darkness. Thanks for being a good husband and a great father. For everything you have done, I love you with all I can. Can't wait to shower you with my affectionate kisses. See you tomorrow."

He then searched for appropriate emojis, but he locked his phone and placed it on the table as he reached the stage. The crowd eagerly awaited him, and he felt overwhelmed with emotion, eager to express his gratitude for their affection and unwavering support.

As he made his way towards the dazzling fog lights, a surge of excitement and nervous anticipation coursed through him. The brilliant lights momentarily dazzled his vision, but the deafening applause that erupted from every corner of the theater filled his soul with an intoxicating elation. Taking a deep breath, he stood tall, humbled by the outpouring of love and support from the adoring audience.

With a gracious bow, he expressed his heartfelt gratitude, acknowledging the immense impact they had created. Maya, Bejoy, and the rest of the artists stood behind him, forming a united front. With beaming smiles and hearts filled with pride, they gracefully bowed to the audience. The camaraderie and shared journey of triumph were evident in their actions, as they acknowledged the collective efforts that had brought them to this memorable moment.

In that surreal moment, the cacophony of cheers and roars surrounded him, yet a profound sense of clarity washed over Apu. Amidst the glimmering glamor and the accolades, he realized that this was not just another performance—it was a celebration of his journey, of his triumphs and tribulations, and most importantly, the acceptance of his true self. Apu's heart swelled with pride and joy as he embraced the realization that he had finally found his light. This newfound self-awareness and authenticity were more precious than any accolade or fame he had ever sought.

With a renewed sense of purpose, Apu stepped into the spotlight once again, basking in the affectionate looks of the crowd. In that radiant moment, he knew he was no longer just an actor playing a part; he was living his truth, unapologetically embracing who he was, and relishing the joy of being authentically himself. The applause and cheers continued to echo, resonating in his heart long after the curtains fell. And he took his final bow.

XIX

Later that night, Yaqoob and his wife invited me to his place for dinner. I could smell the delicious aroma of food as I walked into their house. I expected a small house, but I was surprised to find that it was smaller than I had imagined. The living space was cramped and the kitchen was tiny. Despite its size, it was full of life.

Yaqoob spread the different dishes on the floor mat. The electricity had turned out and we were left with a single orange bulb hanging in the corner of the room that spread ethereal light throughout the place. I could feel a chill in the air as I sat cross-legged on the floor with my back against the wall. Opposite me was a window, providing a view of the entire burial ground. As I stared into its emptiness, a little girl filled the space with her enchanting presence. She then placed a bowl of meat on the floor and the scent wafted through the air, providing a pleasant distraction from the solemn atmosphere.

It was impossible not to smile when I saw her. She waved back at me before running into the kitchen, where her mother passed on her food. She returned shortly after with a jug of water, placing it beside me before sitting down with her father. We all sat in comfortable silence, taking in the beauty of the moment.

I savored every bite of the food that Yaqoob served me. His wife cooked some of the most delicious dishes I had ever tasted. The aroma of steamed rice, the tenderness of the mutton korma, and the perfectly cooked chicken gravy were all delightful. I smiled at his wife as she stood at the entrance of the kitchen, proud of her cooking. I couldn't remember the last time I had enjoyed such a meal for dinner. It was truly a culinary delight.

I asked Yaqoob about the luggage and plastic bags next to me.

"My wife works at a tea estate a few kilometers from here. It's difficult for her to travel every day, so she stays there and visits us every fifteen days. Or we would travel to the property where she works once in a while. Pari loves the place." Yaqoob replied, and as he looked into Pari's eyes, he leaned in and kissed the side of her head.

Pari sat patiently, eagerly awaiting her father to carve the succulent meat off the bone and onto her plate. I kept staring at her often, mesmerized by her beauty. Her long, dark brown hair was pulled up into a tiny bun, and her blue eyes sparkled against her smooth, brown skin. She was stunning! As the meat was finally placed on her plate, her eyes lit up with excitement and a smile spread across her face.

"Do you know we live in a house filled with stars?" The little girl whispered as she munched on her rice ball.

"Woah, where is it?" I attempted to emulate her innocent, childish tone as I spoke to her, hoping to encourage her to continue the conversation.

"It's in the house itself." Her eyes were not confined to one place or object, but swept all around her.

"Where is it? I don't see any stars?"

"Papa, can I turn off the light to show him the stars?" She asked her father.

Pari felt relief as her father approved. She cautiously stepped forward and reached for the switch. In one swift motion she flicked it off and the room was plunged into darkness. She stood there for a while.

"Where is it? There are no stars here." I looked up at the ceiling, unsure of what she was trying to show me.

"You are looking at the wrong place all this time. Turn around, the stars are just behind you." She pointed at the wall, her fingers outstretched. I leaned against it, my weight resting on the rough surface.

The wall behind me entranced me. It was filled with radiant green star-like stickers that glittered in the dim light. She gave me a different perspective on something I had never thought of before. I began to slowly run my fingers through the stars, feeling the texture of each one of them. It was like I had been transported to a different world, one of beauty and wonder. I heard her voice again and it was like a revelation.

She turned on the lights and ran into her kitchen. Yaqoob was delighted to see his daughter's excitement at having a guest at their house. Pari held a glass jar close to her chest, filled with folded bits of paper.

"What are those papers in the jar?" I asked her, trying to look surprised. I turned my gaze away from the walls, which were so radiant that they almost made me forget why I was there in the first place.

"This is all I want to do with my life. Papa has asked me to write it down and put it here whenever I get another wish. It is so that he can help me achieve them one by one when I grow up." She smiled, displaying the hollow spaces between her teeth.

She put the jar down and walked back to her spot. I glanced over to Yaqoob and he gave me a friendly smile in return. Our eyes met for a moment and we both returned to eating our meals.

After dinner, I stepped out and observed the torrential rain. My attention was then drawn to Yaqoob and his daughter. The puppies cried in the rain, so Yaqoob passed them to Pari, and she collected them safely and put them in their house. Yaqoob then walked out and sat next to me, but I kept looking at her daughter's smile.

"That's your grave." I followed the direction he pointed and saw a shovel stuck in the soil.

"I have kept a white bottle next to your bed. It will help you sleep well."

He kept his head down, looking straight ahead, fixed on the graveyard. The grassy grounds were still and quiet, save for crickets chirping.

"You have a beautiful family." I scanned around the small space they called home, and it was filled with more joy than I had ever experienced.

"It's all because of her... My daughter." As Yaqoob watched his daughter sleep the puppies, he said, "She brings all the blessings."

"She looks beautiful. Like an angel."

"She is our goddess." Yaqoob sighed in deep emotion. His eyes overflowed with love and admiration.

"Few days back, I felt the same way about a woman. It was Simran." I held the cigarette between my fingers and offered him the box. He shook his head and turned away.

"And yet you fucked her." Yaqoob had a peculiar smile on his face as he stared at me, with his head leaning against the pillar behind him.

I felt the weight of my mistakes as I stood there, stupefied. Taking a deep breath, I reached for the cigarette I had taken and placed it back where it belonged.

"But you too seek pleasure from Simran." I fired back.

As he smirked, I felt a sense of confusion and unease. I didn't understand his smile, but I could feel it was directed at me. It was as if he was looking down on me, pitying me for something I didn't even know about. It made me feel small and insignificant, like I didn't belong in his world.

"A few months ago, a man came to this place, like you have. He seemed to be in a state of profound despair and hopelessness, like a shattered mirror that could not be put back together. I tried my efforts to console him and offer him words of encouragement, but he would become angry and lash out, even hitting me. His last words to me were 'This world is cruel,' and later that evening I buried him right there." Yaqoob pointed to a grave by nodding his chin and gazing in its direction. Despite his indication, I struggled to identify the exact location of the grave, as darkness concealed the markers and made them indistinguishable.

"After burying him, sadness overwhelmed me. It was like a heavy burden on my chest that I couldn't shake off. As I glanced around, I noticed a few lilac flowers scattered on the ground. It was summertime, and the fallen flowers looked out of place, as if they didn't belong in the vast and lively graveyard surroundings. They were shed and appeared sad and alone, as if they mourned the loss of their companions. Few minutes later, my wife walked over and picked the lilacs, forming a string of beautiful violet flowers out of them. She then placed them on my daughter's hair, who was playing nearby. They looked so lovely on her hair, and I couldn't help but feel warmth and contentment. This simple moment made me realize that sometimes we all need to wait for that person or something we love to lift us up. This will place us where we belong. And if that moment doesn't occur, maybe we should wait. So we could give meaning to this life. Hope lives forever; you just need to find out where." He looked straight into my eyes and smiled at me, his eyes sparkling with a glint, and again rested his head on the pillar against him.

"One may empathize with another person's pain and suffering, but it is impossible to truly feel their emotions as they do. For some of us, the pursuit of love, passion, and hope can feel like a never-ending race. We run tirelessly, convinced that with each step we are closer to our goals, our dreams. Yet, after years of running, we may suddenly be forced to stop and reflect on our journey. It is in this moment of reflection that we may realize we have been running on a one-way road, headed in the wrong direction all along. Looking forward, we may see only a narrow, endless void path. And behind us is a long list of regrets." I kept staring at the shovel stuck in my grave and could feel Yaqoob's gaze in my eyes.

"Someone like me can never find those lilacs. Happiness has a symphony that I could not hear anymore. Sadness weeps, and it echoes in my head all the time. Life is not a lilac for everyone." I patted his shoulder and smiled at him.

He heard his daughter calling from inside and rose to his feet. As he walked by, he said "I have kept a lantern under your table. You may need that to use the bathroom."

I stood at the entrance quiet and still, watching him play with Pari and the puppies. As I watched the scene unfold, my feet slowly carried me away into the rain. I felt the raindrops on my skin, each like a needle stabbing me. I silently bowed my head and walked back to my room.

Night is a time for contemplating the tangle of thoughts that encircle my mind like an intricate circuit. As I gazed at my own grave, I found myself wondering whether any of the strangers I've crossed paths with will recall me once I'm no longer here. Just as I remember the lady who sold vegetables, her stall visible from the window of my apartment, her spot and produce perpetually reserved. She was larger in size, appearing to battle obesity, likely weighing well over 100 kgs. Stationary at her post, she remained a fixture, even resting beside her vegetables under a tarpaulin at night. I became accustomed to observing her life and contemplating her backstory; this routine became a part of my everyday life once. I often pondered her tale – did she possess a family? Why had she been forsaken? What compelled her to sleep on the streets?

One evening, I discovered her spot empty. Though we'd never exchanged words, an inexplicable emptiness gripped my heart, a hollowness surpassing the vacancy she left behind. Yet, the point isn't about the lady, but this world.

The world is currently in the midst of a bizarre revolution, where a particular group savors the diverse culinary pleasures, alongside I observe boys selling pens amidst traffic and elders weep on the streets, their eyes heavy with emotion and skin weathered by time, all in pursuit of a single daily meal to sustain their families. Amidst this, luxury cars illuminate the streets, yet I also witness a spike in homeless people crafting their own tiny beautiful world within the boundaries of just fifteen terracotta pavement tiles. Patriotism finds its outlet through sports and activities, often manipulating the youth with exaggerated displays of loyalty, leading them to unleash needless anger at every opportunity. Strangely, within this very world, the prevalence of wars, disdain for the underprivileged, biases, and honor killings are on a troubling rise.

Yet, the point isn't merely about right versus wrong, good or bad. I hold no opposition against any groups, for I've sailed on both vessels, adrift toward an uncertain destination, much like a bewildered traveler. At times, I strive to rescue the world, yet countless nights are consumed by my own battle to free myself from my thoughts. Nonetheless, we're all mere hypocrites, inhabiting the minuscule realm of atoms and molecules known as Earth. I stand as one amongst the observing hypocrites, floating without answers in my head. A world without wildlife. A bird with no wings. A lion who forgets to roar. A movie without sounds. That is what a person becomes when they possess extensive knowledge about the universe but fail to understand themselves. I have failed to realize what my soul really craves, which makes me feel like nothing but a forager wherever I go, stay, or take a shit.

But what's the point of it all? Does it lie in death or the accumulation of memories, living fueled by hope? And what can a person pursue if hope crumbles within their grasp? Is it a crime to shake hands with death, or is it unlawful to subsist on false hope?

At times like these, my sorrows embrace death. Why does this notion bring me tranquility? Death, Am I the sole individual in this universe, presently dreaming of resting upright in a grave, the cushion like soil pressed against my body? I yearn for the silence the grave promises, a respite from the cacophony that emanates from every street corner. A silence I have long begged for.

I lit my cigarette and accepted what was about to come. Placed the metal chair at the entrance of my room and stared at the shovel stuck to my grave. I then noticed the white bottle Yaqoob had placed on my table and my eyes were fixed on it for a long time. I tried to stay awake, but eventually succumbed to exhaustion and slept as I sat there.

When I woke up, the rain stopped pouring. It was one o'clock in the night, and I knew I wouldn't be able to sleep with all the thoughts racing through my mind. I slowly opened my car door and reached for the papers in the back seat. I grabbed the chair and lantern from under the bed and settled near my grave.

The view was pleasant and the weather was comfortable. A few stars glistened in the night sky darkness. The air was still and calm, a deep silence enveloping the place. The sound of the wind blowing through the trees was the only sound that broke the silence. I had the urge to write down all the thoughts in my head, as if I couldn't keep them any longer. The papers were spread out in front of me, ready to be filled with words. My soul was filled with emotions that had to be released.

The wind picked up, sending the leaves swirling around me in a frenzied dance. I watched as a piece of paper from my diary broke free from my grasp and flew away in the wind. It fluttered and danced before coming to a gentle rest inside the open grave that had been dug out for me. I took a deep breath and began writing another story.

About Author

As a dynamic blend of a passionate writer and a seasoned Tech professional, Taher Ahmed seamlessly weaves creativity and technical acumen into every endeavor. With a quiver of words and a knack for technology, he traverses the boundaries of imagination and innovation.

Beyond the realm of code, Taher Ahmed's heart beats to the rhythm of cinematic tales. An avid film enthusiast, he finds solace and inspiration in the magic of storytelling on the silver screen. This love for narratives has kindled an innate ability to infuse the written word with the same captivating essence found in his favorite films.

By day, he delves into the world of algorithms and software architecture, sculpting digital landscapes with precision. By night, he transforms into an aspiring writer, crafting stories that ignite the imagination and stir the soul. This dual identity not only showcases his versatility but also the unwavering commitment to creative expression.

With his unique blend of technical prowess and a fervent love for storytelling, he is poised to make a distinctive mark on the Writing landscape. As he embarks on this literary and cinematic journey, Taher Ahmed is excited to collaborate with like-minded individuals who share their passion for innovation and narrative magic.

www.ingramcontent.com/pod-product-compliance
Lightning Source LLC
Chambersburg PA
CBHW062211150726
47991CB00006B/2230
9798891331754